Bret Harte

Mr. Jack Hamlin's Mediation and Other Stories

Bret Harte

Mr. Jack Hamlin's Mediation and Other Stories

ISBN/EAN: 9783744749992

Printed in Europe, USA, Canada, Australia, Japan

Cover: Foto ©Andreas Hilbeck / pixelio.de

More available books at **www.hansebooks.com**

MR. JACK HAMLIN'S MEDIATION

And Other Stories

BY

BRET HARTE

BOSTON AND NEW YORK
HOUGHTON, MIFFLIN AND COMPANY
The Riverside Press, Cambridge
1899

CONTENTS

AT nightfall it began to rain. The wind arose too, and also began to buffet a small, struggling, nondescript figure, creeping along the trail over the rocky upland meadow towards Rylands's rancho. At times its head was hidden in what appeared to be wings thrown upward from its shoulders; at times its broad-brimmed hat was cocked jauntily on one side, and again the brim was fixed over the face like a visor. At one moment a drifting misshapen mass of drapery, at the next its vague garments, beaten back hard against the figure, revealed outlines far too delicate for that rude enwrapping. For it was Mrs. Rylands herself, in her husband's hat and her " hired man's " old blue army overcoat, returning from the post-office two miles away. The wind continued its aggression until she reached the front door of her newly plastered farmhouse, and then a heavier blast shook the pines above the low-pitched, shingled roof, and sent a shower of arrowy drops after her like a Parthian parting, as she entered. She threw aside the overcoat and hat, and somewhat inconsistently entered the sitting-room, to walk to the window and look back upon the path she had just traversed. The wind and the rain swept down a slope, half meadow, half clearing, — a mile away, — to a fringe of sycamores. A mile further lay the stage road, where, three hours later, her husband would alight on his return from Sacramento. It would be a long wet walk for Joshua Rylands, as their only horse had been borrowed by a neighbor.

In that fading light Mrs. Rylands's oval cheek was shining still from the raindrops, but there was something in the expression of her worried face that might have as readily suggested tears. She was strikingly handsome, yet quite as incongruous an ornament to her surroundings as she had been to her outer wrappings a moment ago. Even the clothes she now stood in hinted an inadaptibility to the weather — the house — the position she occupied in it. A figured silk dress, spoiled rather than overworn, was still of a quality inconsistent with her evident habits, and the lace-edged petticoat that peeped beneath it was draggled with mud and unaccustomed usage. Her glossy black hair, which had been tossed into curls in some foreign fashion, was now wind-blown into a burlesque of it. This incongruity was still further accented by the appearance of the room she had entered. It was coldly and severely furnished, making the chill of the yet damp white plaster unpleasantly obvious. A black harmonium organ stood in one corner, set out with black and white hymn-books ; a trestle-like table contained a large Bible ; half a dozen black, horsehair-cushioned chairs stood, geometrically distant, against the walls, from which hung four engravings of " Paradise Lost " in black mourning frames ; some dried ferns and autumn leaves stood in a vase on the mantel-piece, as if the chill of the room had prematurely blighted them. The coldly glittering grate below was also decorated with withered sprays, as if an attempt had been made to burn them, but was frustrated through damp. Suddenly recalled to a sense of her wet boots and the new carpet, she hurriedly turned away, crossed the hall into

the dining-room, and thence passed into the
kitchen. The "hired girl," a large-boned
Missourian, a daughter of a neighboring
woodman, was peeling potatoes at the table.
Mrs. Rylands drew a chair before the kitchen
stove, and put her wet feet on the hob.

"I'll bet a cooky, Mess Rylands, you've
done forgot the vanillar," said the girl, with a
certain domestic and confidential familiarity.

Mrs. Rylands started guiltily. She made
a miserable feint of looking in her lap and
on the table. "I'm afraid I did, Jane, if
I didn't bring it in *here*."

"That you didn't," returned Jane. "And
I reckon ye forgot that 'ar pepper-sauce for
yer husband."

Mrs. Rylands looked up with piteous con-
trition. "I really don't know what's the
matter with me. I certainly went into the
shop, and had it on my list, — and —
really " —

Jane evidently knew her mistress, and
smiled with superior toleration. "It's
kinder bewilderin' goin' in them big shops,
and lookin' round them stuffed shelves."
The shop at the cross roads and post-office
was 14 × 14, but Jane was nurtured on the

plains. "Anyhow," she added good-humoredly, "the expressman is sure to look in as he goes by, and you've time to give him the order."

"But is he *sure* to come?" asked Mrs. Rylands anxiously. "Mr. Rylands will be so put out without his pepper-sauce."

"He's sure to come ef he knows you're here. Ye kin always kalkilate on that."

"Why?" said Mrs. Rylands abstractedly.

"Why? 'cause he just can't keep his eyes off ye! That's why he comes every day,— 't ain't jest for trade!"

This was quite true, not only of the expressman, but of the butcher and baker, and the "candlestick-maker," had there been so advanced a vocation at the cross roads. All were equally and curiously attracted by her picturesque novelty. Mrs. Rylands knew this herself, but without vanity or coquettishness. Possibly that was why the other woman told her. She only slightly deepened the lines of discontent in her cheek and said abstractedly, "Well, when he comes, *you* ask him."

She dried her shoes, put on a pair of slippers that had a faded splendor about them, and went up to her bedroom. Here she hesitated for some time between the sewing-machine and her knitting-needles, but finally settled upon the latter, and a pair of socks for her husband which she had begun à year ago. But she presently despaired of finishing them before he returned, three hours hence, and so applied herself to the sewing-machine. For a little while its singing hum was heard between the blasts that shook the house, but the thread presently snapped, and the machine was put aside somewhat impatiently, with a discontented drawing of the lines around her handsome mouth. Then she began to "tidy" the room, putting a great many things away and bringing out a great many more, a process that was necessarily slow, owing to her falling into attitudes of minute inspection of certain articles of dress, with intervals of trying them on, and observing their effect in her mirror. This kind of interruption also occurred while she was putting away some books that were lying about on chairs and tables, stopping midway to open their pages, becoming interested, and quite finishing one chapter, with the book held close against the window to catch the fading light of day. The feminine reader will gather from this that Mrs. Rylands, though charming, was not facile in domestic duties. She had just glanced at the clock, and lit the candle to again set herself to work, and thus bridge over the two hours more of waiting, when there came a tap at the door. She opened it to Jane.

"There's an entire stranger downstairs, ez hez got a lame hoss and wants to borry a fresh one."

"We have none, you know," said Mrs. Rylands, a little impatiently.

"Thet's what I told him. Then he wanted to know ef he could lie by here till he could get one or fix up his own hoss."

"As you like; you know if you can manage it," said Mrs. Rylands, a little uneasily. "When Mr. Rylands comes you can arrange it between you. Where is he now?"

"In the kitchen."

"The kitchen!" echoed Mrs. Rylands.

"Yes, ma'am, I showed him into the parlor, but he kinder shivered his shoulders, and reckoned ez how he'd go inter the kitchen. Ye see, ma'am, he was all wet, and his shiny big boots was sloppy. But he ain't one o' the stuck-up kind, and he's willin' to make hisself comf'ble before the kitchen stove."

"Well, then, he don't want *me*," said Mrs. Rylands, with a relieved voice.

"Yes'm," said Jane, apparently equally relieved. "Only, I thought I'd just tell you."

A few minutes later, in crossing the upper hall, Mrs. Rylands heard Jane's voice from the kitchen raised in rustic laughter. Had she been satirically inclined, she might have understood Jane's willingness to relieve her mistress of the duty of entertaining the stranger; had she been philosophical, she might have considered the girl's dreary, monotonous life at the rancho, and made allowance for her joy at this rare interruption of it. But I fear that Mrs. Rylands was neither satirical nor philosophical, and presently, when Jane reëntered, with color in her alkaline face, and light in her huckleberry eyes, and said she was going over to the cattle-sheds in the "far pasture," to see if the hired man did n't know of some horse that could be got for the stranger, Mrs. Rylands felt a little bitterness in the thought that the girl would have scarcely volunteered to go all that distance in the rain for *her*. Yet, in a few moments she forgot all about it, and even the presence of her guest in the house, and in one of her fitful abstracted employments passed through the dining-room into the kitchen, and had opened the door with an " Oh, Jane! " before she remembered her absence.

The kitchen, lit by a single candle, could be only partly seen by her as she stood with her hand on the lock, although she herself was plainly visible. There was a pause, and then a quiet, self-possessed, yet amused, voice answered : —

" My name is n't Jane, and if you 're the lady of the house, I reckon yours was n't *always* Rylands."

At the sound of the voice Mrs. Rylands threw the door wide open, and as her eyes fell upon the speaker — her unknown guest — she recoiled with a little cry, and a white, startled face. Yet the stranger was young and handsome, dressed with a scrupulousness and elegance which even the stress of travel had not deranged, and he was looking at her with a smile of recognition, mingled

with that careless audacity and self-possession which seemed to be the characteristic
of his face.

"Jack Hamlin!" she gasped.

"That's me, all the time," he responded
easily, "and *you're* Nell Montgomery!"

"How did you know I was here? Who
told you?" she said impetuously.

"Nobody! never was so surprised in my
life! When you opened that door just
now you might have knocked me down with
a feather." Yet he spoke lazily, with an
amused face, and looked at her without
changing his position.

"But you *must* have known *something!*
It was no mere accident," she went on
vehemently, glancing around the room.

"That's where you slip up, Nell," said
Hamlin imperturbably. "It *was* an accident and a bad one. My horse lamed himself coming down the grade. I sighted the
nearest shanty, where I thought I might get
another horse. It happened to be this."
For the first time he changed his attitude,
and leaned back contemplatively in his
chair.

She came towards him quickly. "You

did n't use to lie, Jack," she said hesitatingly.

" Could n't afford it in my business, — and can't now," said Jack cheerfully. " But," he · added curiously, as if recognizing something in his companion's agitation, and lifting his brown lashes to her, the window, and the ceiling, " what 's all this about ? What 's your little game here ? "

" I 'm married," she said, with nervous intensity, — " married, and this is my husband's house ! "

" Not married straight out! — regularly fixed ? "

" Yes," she said hurriedly.

" One of the boys? Don't remember any Rylands. *Spelter* used to be very sweet on you, — but Spelter might n't have been his real name ? "

" None of our lot! No one you ever knew; a — a straight out, square man," she said quickly.

" I say, Nell, look here ! You ought to have shown up your cards without even a call. You ought to have told him that you danced at the Casino."

" I did."

" Before he asked you to marry him ? "

" Before."

Jack got up from his chair, put his hands in his pockets, and looked at her curiously. This Nell Montgomery, this music-hall " dance and song girl," this girl of whom so much had been *said* and so little *proved !* Well, this was becoming interesting.

" You don't understand," she said, with nervous feverishness ; " you remember after that row I had with Jim, that night the manager gave us a supper, — when he treated me like a dog ? "

" He did that," interrupted Jack.

" I felt fit for anything," she said, with a half-hysterical laugh, that seemed voiced, however, to check some slumbering memory. " I'd have cut my throat or his, it did n't matter which " —

" It mattered something to us, Nell," put in Jack again, with polite parenthesis ; " don't leave *us* out in the cold."

" I started from 'Frisco that night on the boat ready to fling myself into anything — or the river ! " she went on hurriedly. " There was a man in the cabin who noticed me, and began to hang around. I thought he knew who I was, — had seen me on the posters ; and as I did n't feel like foolin', I told him so. But he was n't that kind. He said he saw I was in trouble and wanted me to tell him all."

Mr. Hamlin regarded her cheerfully. " And you told him," he said, " how you had once run away from your childhood's happy home to go on the stage ! How you always regretted it, and would have gone back but that the doors were shut forever against you ! How you longed to leave, but the wicked men and women around you always " —

" I did n't ! " she burst out, with sudden passion; "you know I did n't. I told him everything : who I was, what I had done, what I expected to do again. I pointed out the men — who were sitting there, whispering and grinning at us, as if they were in the front row of the theatre — and said I knew them all, and they knew me. I never spared myself a thing. I said what people said of me, and did n't even care to say it was n't true ! "

" Oh, come ! " protested Jack, in perfunctory politeness.

" He said he liked me for telling the

truth, and not being ashamed to do it! He
said the sin was in the false shame and the
hypocrisy; for that's the sort of man he is,
you see, and that's like him always! He
asked if I would marry him — out of hand
— and do my best to be his lawful wife.
He said he wanted me to think it over and
sleep on it, and to-morrow he would come
and see me for an answer. I slipped off the
boat at 'Frisco, and went alone to a hotel
where I was n't known. In the morning I
did n't know whether he'd keep his word or
I'd keep mine. But he came! He said
he'd marry me that very day, and take me
to his farm in Santa Clara. I agreed. I
thought it would take me out of everybody's
knowledge, and they'd think me dead! We
were married that day, before a regular
clergyman. I was married under my own
name," — she stopped and looked at Jack,
with a hysterical laugh, — " but he made me
write underneath it, ' known as Nell ·Mont-
gomery;' for he said *he* was n't ashamed of
it, nor should I be."

" Does he wear long hair and stick straws
in it?" said Hamlin gravely. " Does he
' hear voices ' and have ' visions '?"

" He's a shrewd, sensible, hard-working
man, — no more mad than you are, nor as
mad as *I* was the day I married him. He's
lived up to everything he's said." She
stopped, hesitated in her quick, nervous
speech ; her lip quivered slightly, but she
recalled herself, and looking imploringly,
yet hopelessly, at Jack, gasped, " And that's
what's the matter ! "

Jack fixed his eyes keenly upon her.
" And you ? " he said curtly.

" I ? " she repeated wonderingly.

" Yes, what have *you* done ? " he said,
with sudden sharpness.

The wonder was so apparent in her eyes
that his keen glance softened. " Why,"
she said bewilderingly, " I have been his
dog, his slave, — as far as he would let me.
I have done everything ; I have not been
out of the house until he almost drove me
out. I have never wanted to go anywhere
or see any one ; but he has always insisted
upon it. I would have been willing to slave
here, day and night, and have been happy.
But he said I must not seem to be ashamed
of my past, when he is not. I would have
worn common homespun clothes and calico

frocks, and been glad of it, but he insists upon my wearing my best things, even my theatre things ; and as he can't afford to buy more, I wear these things I had. I know they look beastly here, and that I'm a laughing-stock, and when I go out I wear almost anything to try and hide them ; but," her lip quivered dangerously again, " he wants me to do it, and it pleases him."

Jack looked down. After a pause he lifted his lashes towards her draggled skirt, and said in an easier, conversational tone, " Yes! I thought I knew that dress. *I* gave it to you for that walking scene in ' High Life,' did n't I ? "

" No," she said quickly, " it was the blue one with silver trimming, — don't you remember? I tried to turn it the first year I was married, but it never looked the same."

" It was sweetly pretty," said Jack encouragingly, " and with that blue hat lined with silver, it was just fetching ! Somehow I don't quite remember this one," and he looked at it critically.

" I had it at the races in '58, and that supper Judge Boompointer gave us at 'Frisco where Colonel Fish upset the table trying to get at Jim. Do you know," she said, with a little laugh, " it's got the stains of the champagne on it yet; it never would come off. See!" and she held the candle with great animation to the breadth of silk before her.

" And there's more of it on the sleeve," said Jack; " is n't there?"

Mrs. Rylands looked reproachfully at Jack.

" That is n't champagne; don't you know what it is?"

" No!"

" It's blood," she said gravely; " when that Mexican cut poor Ned so bad, — don't you remember? I held his head upon my arm while you bandaged him." She heaved a little sigh, and then added, with a faint laugh, " That's the worst thing about the clothes of a girl in the profession, they get spoiled or stained before they wear out."

This large truth did not seem to impress Mr. Hamlin. " Why did you leave Santa Clara?" he said abruptly, in his previous critical tone.

" Because of the folks there. They were standoffish and ugly. You see, Josh " —

" Who ? "

" Josh Rylands ! — *him !* He told everybody who I was, even those who had never
seen me in the bills, — how good I was to
marry him, how he had faith in me and
was n't ashamed, — until they did n't believe
we were married at all. So they looked
another way when they met us, and did n't
call. And all the while I was glad they
did n't, but he would n't believe it, and
allowed I was pining on account of it."

" And were you ? "

" I swear to God, Jack, I 'd have been
content, and more, to have been just there
with him, seein' nobody, letting every one
believe I was dead and gone, but he said it
was wrong, and weak! Maybe it was," she
added, with a shy, interrogating look at
Jack, of which, however, he took no notice.
" Then when he found they would n't call,
what do you think he did ? "

" Beat you, perhaps," suggested Jack
cheerfully.

" He never did a thing to me that was n't
straight out, square, and kind," she said,
half indignantly, half hopelessly. " He
thought if *his* kind of people would n't see

me, I might like to see my own sort. So
without saying anything to me, he brought
down, of all things! Tinkie Clifford, she
that used to dance in the cheap variety
shows at 'Frisco, and her particular friend,
Captain Sykes. It would have just killed
you, Jack," she said, with a sudden hysteric
burst of laughter, " to have seen Josh, in his
square, straight-out way, trying to be civil
and help things along. But," she went on,
as suddenly relapsing into her former attitude of worried appeal, " *I* could n't stand
it, and when she got to talking free and
easy before Josh, and Captain Sykes to guz-
zling champagne, she and me had a row.
She allowed I was putting on airs, and I
made her walk, in spite of Josh."

" And Josh seemed to like it," said Hamlin carelessly.. " Has he seen her since ? "

" No ; I reckon he 's cured of asking that
kind of company for me. And then we
came here. But I persuaded him not to
begin by going round telling people who I
was, — as he did the last time, — but to
leave it to folks to find out if they wanted
to, and he gave in. Then he let me fix up
this house and furnish it my own way, and
I did ! "

"Do you mean to say that *you* fixed up that family vault of a sitting-room?" said Jack, in horror.

"Yes, I did n't want any fancy furniture or looking-glasses, and such like, to attract folks, nor anything to look like the old times. I don't think any of the boys would care to come here. And I got rid of a lot of sporting travelers, 'wild-cat' managers, and that kind of tramp in this way. But" — She hesitated, and her face fell again.

"But what?" said Jack.

"I don't think that Josh likes it either. He brought home the other day 'My Johnny is a Shoemakiyure,' and wanted me to try it on the organ. But it reminded me how we used to get just sick of singing it on and off the boards, and I could n't touch it. He wanted me to go to the circus that was touring over at the cross roads, but it was the old Flanigin's circus, you know, the one Gussie Riggs used to ride in, with its old clown and its old ringmaster and the old 'wheezes,' and I chucked it."

"Look here," said Jack, rising and surveying Mrs. Rylands critically. "If you go on at this gait, I 'll tell you what that

man of yours will do. He'll bolt with some
of your old friends!"

She turned a quick, scared face upon him
for an instant. But only for an instant.
Her hysteric little laugh returned at once,
followed by her weary, worried look. "No,
Jack, you don't know him! If it was only
that! He cares only for me in his own
way,—and," she stammered as she went
on, "I've no luck in making him happy."

She stopped. The wind shook the house
and fired a volley of rain against the windows. She took advantage of it to draw
a torn lace-edged handkerchief from her
pocket behind, and keeping the tail of her
eyes in a frightened fashion on Jack, applied
the handkerchief furtively, first to her nose,
and then to her eyes.

"Don't do that," said Jack fastidiously,
"it's wet enough outside." Nevertheless,
he stood up and gazed at her.

"Well," he began.

She timidly drew nearer to him, and took
a seat on the kitchen table, looking up wistfully into his eyes.

"Well," resumed Jack argumentatively,
"if he won't 'chuck' you, why don't you
'chuck' *him?*"

She turned quite white, and suddenly dropped her eyes. "Yes," she said, almost inaudibly, "lots of girls would do that."

"I don't mean go back to your old life," continued Jack. "I reckon you've had enough of that. But get into some business, you know, like other women. A bonnet shop, or a candy shop for children, see? I'll help start you. I've got a couple of hundred, if not in my own pocket in somebody's else, just burning to be used! And then you can look about you; and perhaps some square business man will turn up and you can marry him. You know you can't live this way, nohow. It's killing you; it ain't fair on you, nor on Rylands either."

"No," she said quickly, "it ain't fair on *him*. I know it, I know it isn't, I know it isn't," she repeated, "only"— She stopped.

"Only what?" said Jack impatiently.

She did not speak. After a pause she picked up the rolling-pin from the table and began absently rolling it down her lap to her knee, as if pressing out the stained silk skirt. "Only," she stammered, slowly rolling the pin handles in her open palms, "I —I can't leave Josh."

" Why can't you?" said Jack quickly.

" Because — because — I," she went on, with a quivering lip, working the rolling-pin heavily down her knee as if she were crushing her answer out of it, — "because — I — love him!"

There was a pause, a dash of rain against the window, and another dash from her eyes upon her hands, the rolling-pin, and the skirts she had gathered up hastily, as she cried, "O Jack! Jack! I never loved anybody like him! I never knew what love was! I never knew a man like him before! There never *was* one before!"

To this large, comprehensive, and passionate statement Mr. Jack Hamlin made no reply. An audacity so supreme had conquered his. He walked to the window, looked out upon the dark, rain-filmed pane that, however, reflected no equal change in his own dark eyes, and then returned and walked round the kitchen table. When he was at her back, without looking at her, he reached out his hand, took her passive one that lay on the table in his, grasped it heartily for a single moment, laid it gently down, and returned around the table, where he again confronted her cheerfully face to face.

"You'll make the riffle yet," he said quietly. "Just now I don't see what *I* could do, or where I could chip in your little game; but if I *do*, or you do, count me in and let me know. You know where to write, — my old address at Sacramento." He walked to the corner, took up his still wet serape, threw it over his shoulders, and picked up his broad-brimmed riding-hat.

"You're not going, Jack?" she said hesitatingly, as she rubbed her wet eyes into a consciousness of his movements. "You'll wait to see *him?* He'll be here in an hour."

"I've been here too long already," said Jack. "And the less you say about my calling, even accidentally, the better. Nobody will believe it, — *you* didn't yourself. In fact, unless you see how I can help you, the sooner you consider us all dead and buried, the sooner your luck will change. Tell your girl I've found my own horse so much better that I have pushed on with him, and give her that."

He threw a gold coin on the table.

" But your horse is still lame," she said wonderingly. " What will you do in this storm ? "

" Get into the cover of the next wood and camp out. I 've done it before."

" But, Jack ! "

He suddenly made a slight gesture of warning. His quick ear had caught the approach of footsteps along the wet gravel outside. A mischievous light slid into his dark eyes as he coolly moved backward to the door and, holding it open, said, in a remarkably clear and distinct voice : —

" Yes, as you say, society is becoming very mixed and frivolous everywhere, and you 'd scarcely know San Francisco now. So delighted, however, to have made your acquaintance, and regret my business prevents my waiting to see your good husband. So odd that I should have known your Aunt Jemima ! But, as you say, the world is very small, after all. I shall tell the Deacon how well you are looking, — in spite of the kitchen smoke in your eyes. Good-by ! A thousand thanks for your hospitality."

And Jack, bowing profoundly to the ground, backed out upon Jane, the hired

man, and the expressman, treading, I grieve
to say, with some deliberation upon the toes
of the two latter, in order, possibly, that
in their momentary pain and discomposure
they might not scan too closely the face of
this ingenious gentleman, as he melted into
the night and the storm.

Jane entered, with a slight, toss of her
head.

"Here's your expressman, — ef you're
wantin' him *now*."

Mrs. Rylands was too preoccupied to
notice her handmaiden's significant emphasis, as she indicated a fresh-looking, bashful
young fellow, whose confusion was evidently
heightened by the unexpected egress of Mr.
Hamlin, and the point-blank presence of the
handsome Mrs. Rylands.

"Oh, certainly," said Mrs. Rylands
quickly. "So kind of him to oblige us.
Give him the order, Jane, please."

She turned to escape from the kitchen
and these new intruders, when her eye fell
upon the coin left by Mr. Hamlin. "The
gentleman wished you to take that for your
trouble, Jane," she said hastily, pointing to
it, and passed out.

Jane cast a withering look after her re-
treating skirts, and picking the coin from
the table, turned to the hired man. "Run
to the stable after that dandified young
feller, Dick, and hand that back to him.
Ye kin say that Jane Mackinnon don't run
arrants fur money, nor play gooseberry to
other folks fur fun."

PART II

MR. JOSHUA RYLANDS had, according to
the vocabulary of his class, "found grace"
at the age of sixteen, while still in the spiritual state of "original sin" and the political
one of Missouri. He had not indeed found
it by persistent youthful seeking or spiritual
insight, but somewhat violently and turbu-
lently at a camp-meeting. A village boy,
naturally gentle and impressible, with an
original character, — limited, however, in
education and experience, — he had, after
his first rustic debauch with some vulgar
companions, fallen upon the camp-meeting
in reckless audacity; and instead of being
handed over to the district constable, was
taken in and placed upon "the anxious

bench," " rastled with," and exhorted by
a strong revivalist preacher, "convicted of
sin," and — converted ! It is doubtful if
the shame of a public arrest and legal pun-
ishment would have impressed his youthful
spirit as much as did this spiritual examination and trial, in which he himself became
accuser. Howbeit, its effect, though puni-
tive, was also exemplary. He at once cast
off his evil companions; remaining faithful
to his conversion, in spite of their later
" backslidings." When, after the Western
fashion, the time came for him to forsake
his father's farm and seek a new " quarter
section " on some more remote frontier, he
carried into that secluded, lonely, half-
monkish celibacy of pioneer life — which
has been the foundation of so much strong
Western character — more than the usual
religious feeling. At once industrious and
adventurous, he lived by " the Word," as he
called it, and Nature as he knew it, — tempted
by none of the vices or sentiments of civilization. When he finally joined the Californian
emigration, it was not as a gold-seeker, but
as a discoverer of new agricultural fields; if
the hardship was as great and the rewards

fewer, he nevertheless knew that he retained his safer isolation and independence of spirit. Vice and civilization were to him synonymous terms; it was the natural condition of the worldly and unregenerate. Such was the man who chanced to meet " Nell Montgomery, the Pearl of the Variety Stage," on the Sacramento boat, in one of his forced visits to civilization. Without knowing her in her profession, her frank exposition of herself did not startle him; he recognized it, accepted it, and strove to convert it. And as long as this daughter of Folly forsook her evil ways for him, it was a triumph in which there was no shame, and might be proclaimed from the housetop. When his neighbors thought differently, and avoided them, he saw no inconsistency in bringing his wife's old friends to divert her: she might in time convert *them.* He had no more fear of her returning to their ways than he had of himself " backsliding." Narrow as was his creed, he had none of the harshness nor pessimism of the bigot. With the keenest self-scrutiny, his credulity regarding others was touching.

The storm was still raging when he

alighted that evening from the up coach at the trail nearest his house. Although incumbered with a heavy carpet-bag, he started resignedly on his two-mile tramp without begrudging the neighborly act of his wife which had deprived him of his horse. It was "like her" to do these things in her good-humored abstraction, an abstraction, however, that sometimes worried him, from the fear that it indicated some unhappiness with her present lot. He was longing to rejoin her after his absence of three days, the longest time they had been separated since their marriage, and he hurried on with a certain lover-like excitement, quite new to his usually calm and temperate blood.

Struggling with the storm and darkness, but always with the happy consciousness of drawing nearer to her in that struggle, he labored on, finding his perilous way over the indistinguishable trail by certain landmarks in the distance, visible only to his pioneer eye. That heavier shadow to the right was not the hillside, but the *slope* to the distant hill; that low, regular line immediately before him was not a fence or wall, but the line of distant gigantic woods,

a mile from his home. Yet as he began
to descend the slope towards the wood, he
stopped and rubbed his eyes. There was
distinctly a light in it. His first idea was
that he had lost the trail and was nearing
the woodman Mackinnon's cabin. But a
more careful scrutiny revealed to him that
it was really the wood, and the light was a
camp-fire. It was a rough night for camping out, but they were probably some belated prospectors.

When he had reached the fringe of woodland, he could see quite plainly that the fire
was built beside one of the large pines, and
that the little encampment, which looked
quite comfortable and secluded from the
storm-beaten trail, was occupied apparently
by a single figure. By the good glow of the
leaping fire, that figure standing erect before
it, elegantly shaped, in the graceful folds of a
serape, looked singularly romantic and picturesque, and reminded Joshua Rylands —
whose ideas of art were purely reminiscent
of boyish reading — of some picture in a
novel. The heavy black columns of the
pines, glancing out of the concave shadow,
also seemed a fitting background to what

might have been a scene in a play. So strongly was he impressed by it that but for his anxiety to reach his home, still a mile distant, and the fact that he was already late, he would have penetrated the wood and the seclusion of the stranger with an offer of hospitality for the night. The man, however, was evidently capable of taking care of himself, and the outline of a tethered horse was faintly visible under another tree. It might be a surveyor or engineer, — the only men of a better class who were itinerant.

But another and even greater surprise greeted him as he toiled up the rocky slope towards his farmhouse. The windows of the sitting-room, which were usually blank and black by night, were glittering with unfamiliar light. Like most farmers, he seldom used the room except for formal company, his wife usually avoiding it, and even he himself now preferred the dining-room or the kitchen. His first suggestion that his wife had visitors gave him a sense of pleasure on her account, mingled, however, with a slight uneasiness of his own which he could not account for. More than that, as he approached nearer he could hear the swell of the organ above the roar of the swaying pines, and the cadences were not of a devotional character. He hesitated for a moment, as he had hesitated at the fire in the woods; yet it was surely his own house! He hurried to the door, opened it; not only the light of the sitting-room streamed into the hall, but the ruddier glow of an actual fire in the disused grate! The familiar dark furniture had been rearranged to catch some of the glow and relieve its sombreness. And his wife, rising from the music-stool, was the room's only occupant!

Mrs. Rylands gazed anxiously and timidly at her husband's astonished face, as he threw off his waterproof and laid down his carpet-bag. Her own face was a little flurried with excitement, and his, half hidden in his tawny beard, and, possibly owing to his self-introspective nature, never spontaneously sympathetic, still expressed only wonder! Mrs. Rylands was a little frightened, It is sometimes dangerous to meddle with a man's habits, even when he has grown weary of them.

" I thought," she began hesitatingly, " that it would be more cheerful for you in here, this stormy evening. I thought you might like to put your wet things to dry in the kitchen, and we could sit here together, after supper, alone."

I am afraid that Mrs. Rylands did not offer all her thoughts. Ever since Mr. Hamlin's departure she had been uneasy and excited, sometimes falling into fits of dejection, and again lighting up into hysterical levity; at other times carefully examining her wardrobe, and then with a sudden impulse rushing downstairs again to give orders for her husband's supper, and to make the extraordinary changes in the sitting-room already noted. Only a few moments before he arrived, she had covertly brought down a piece of music, and put aside the hymn-books, and taken, with a little laugh, a pack of cards from her pocket, which she placed behind the already dismantled vase on the chimney.

" I reckoned you had company, Ellen," he said gravely, kissing her.

" No," she said quickly. " That is," she stopped with a sudden surge of color in her face that startled her, " there was — a man — here, in the kitchen — who had a lame

horse, and who wanted to get a fresh one.
But he went away an hour ago. And he
was n't in this room — at least, after it was
fixed up. So I 've had no company."

She felt herself again blushing at having
blushed, and a little terrified. There was no
reason for it. But for Jack's warning, she
would have been quite ready to tell her husband all. She had never blushed before
him over her past life; why she should now
blush over seeing Jack, of all people! made
her utter a little hysterical laugh. I am
afraid that this experienced little woman
took it for granted that her husband knew
that if Jack or any man had been there as
a clandestine lover, she would not have
blushed at all. Yet with all her experience, she did not know that she had blushed
simply because it was *to* Jack that she had
confessed that she loved the man before her.
Her husband noted the blush as part of her
general excitement. He permitted her to
drag him into the room and seat him before
the hearth, where she sank down on one
knee to pull off his heavy rubber boots.
But he waved her aside at this, pulled them
off with his own hands, and let her take

them to the kitchen and bring back his slippers. By this time a smile had lighted up his hard face. The room was certainly more comfortable and cheerful. Still he was a little worried; was there not in these changes a falling away from the grace of self-abnegation which she had so sedulously practiced?

When supper was served by Jane, in the dull dining-room, Mr. Rylands, had he not been more engaged in these late domestic changes, might have noticed that the Missouri girl waited upon him with a certain commiserating air that was remarkable by its contrast with the frigid ceremonious politeness with which she attended her mistress. It had not escaped Mrs. Rylands, however, who ever since Jack's abrupt departure had noticed this change in the girl's demeanor to herself, and with a woman's intuitive insight of another woman, had fathomed it. The comfortable *tête-à-tête* with Jack, which Jane had looked forward to, Mrs. Rylands had anticipated herself, and then sent him off! When Joshua thanked his wife for remembering the pepper-sauce, and Mrs. Rylands pathetically admitted her

forgetfulness, the head-toss which Jane gave
as she left the room was too marked to be
overlooked by him. Mrs. Rylands gave a
hysterical little laugh. " I am afraid Jane
does n't like my sending away the expressman just after I had also dismissed the
stranger whom she had taken a fancy to,
and left her without company," she said
unwisely.

Mr. Rylands did not laugh. " I reckon,"
he returned slowly, " that Jane must feel
kinder lonely ; she bears all the burden of
our bein' outer the world, without any of our
glory in the cause of it."

Nevertheless, when supper was over, and
the pair were seated in the sitting-room
before the fire, this episode was forgotten.
Mrs. Rylands produced her husband's pipe
and tobacco-pouch. He looked around the
formal walls and hesitated. He had been
in the habit of smoking in the kitchen.

" Why not here ? " said Mrs. Rylands,
with a sudden little note of decision. " Why
should we keep this room only for company
that don't come ? I call it silly."

This struck Mr. Rylands as logical. Be-
sides, undoubtedly the fire had mellowed the

room. After a puff or two he looked at his wife musingly. " Could n't you make yourself one of them cigarettys, as they call 'em? Here's the tobacco, and I'll get you the paper."

" *I could*," she said tentatively. Then suddenly, " What made you think of it? You never saw *me* smoke!"

" No," said Rylands, " but that lady, your old friend, Miss Clifford, does, and I thought *you* might be hankering after it."

" How do you know Tinkie Clifford smokes?" said Mrs. Rylands quickly.

" She lit a cigaretty that day she called."

" I hate it," said Mrs. Rylands shortly.

Mr. Rylands nodded approval, and puffed meditatively.

" Josh, have you seen that girl since?"

" No," said Joshua.

" Nor any other girl like her?"

" No," said Joshua wonderingly. " You see I only got to know her on your account, Ellen, that she might see you."

" Well, don't you do it any more! None of 'em! Promise me!" She leaned forward eagerly in her chair.

" But" Ellen, — her husband began gravely.

" I know what you're going to say, but they can't do me any good, and you can't do them any good as you did *me*, so there ! "

Mr. Rylands was silent, and smiled meditatively.

" Josh ! "

" Yes."

" When you met me that night on the Sacramento boat, and looked at me, did you — did I," she hesitated, — " did you look at me because I had been crying ? "

" I thought you were troubled in spirit, and looked so."

" I suppose I looked worried, of course ; I had no time to change or even fix my hair; I had on that green dress, and it *never* was becoming. And you only spoke to me on account of my awful looks ? "

" I saw only your wrestling soul, Ellen, and I thought you needed comfort and help."

She was silent for a moment, and then, leaning forward, picked up the poker and began to thrust it absently between the bars.

" And if it had been some other girl crying and looking awful, you 'd have spoken to her all the same ? "

This was a new idea to Mr. Rylands, but with most men logic is supreme. " I suppose I would," he said slowly.

" And married her ? " She rattled the bars of the grate with the poker as if to drown the inevitable reply.

Mr. Rylands loved the woman before him, but it pleased him to think that he loved truth better. " If it had been necessary to her salvation, yes," he said.

" Not Tinkie ? " she said suddenly.

" *She* never would have been in your contrite condition."

" Much you know ! Girls like that can cry as well as laugh, just as they want to. Well ! I suppose I *did* look horrid." Nevertheless, she seemed to gain some gratification from her husband's reply, and changed the subject as if fearful of losing that satisfaction by further questioning.

" I tried some of those songs you brought, but I don't think they go well with the harmonium," she said, pointing to some music on its rack, " except one. Just listen." She rose, and with the same nervous quickness she had shown before, went to the instrument and began to sing and play. There was a hopeless incongruity between the character of the instrument and the spirit of the song. Mrs. Rylands's voice was rather forced and crudely trained, but Joshua Rylands, sitting there comfortably slippered by the fire and conscious of the sheeted rain against the window, felt it good. Presently he arose, and lounging heavily over to the fair performer, leaned down and imprinted a kiss on the labyrinthine fringes of her hair. At which Mrs. Rylands caught blindly at his hand nearest her, and without lifting her other hand from the keys, or her eyes from the music, said tentatively : —

" You know there's a chorus just here! Why can't you try it with me ? "

Mr. Rylands hesitated a moment, then, with a preliminary cough, lifted a voice as crude as hers, but powerful through much camp-meeting exercise, and roared a chorus which was remarkable chiefly for requiring that archness and playfulness in execution which he lacked. As the whole house seemed to dilate with the sound, and the wind outside to withhold its fury, Mr. Rylands felt that physical delight which children feel in personal outcry, and was grateful to his wife for the opportunity.   Laying his hand affectionately on her shoulder, he noticed for the first time that she was in a kind of evening-dress, and that her delicate white shoulder shone through the black lace that enveloped it.

For an instant Mr. Rylands was shocked at this unwonted exposure.   He had never seen his wife in evening-dress before.   It was true they were alone, and in their own sitting-room, but the room was still invested with that formality and publicity which seemed to accent this indiscretion.   The simple-minded frontier man's mind went back to Jane, to the hired man, to the expressman, the stranger, all of whom might have noticed it also.

"You have a new dress," he said slowly, "have you worn it all day?"

"No," she said, with a timid smile.   "I only put it on just before you came.   It's the one I used to wear in the ballroom scene in 'Gay Times in 'Frisco.'   You don't know it, I know.   I thought I would wear it to-night, and then," she suddenly grasped his hand, "you'll let me put all these things away forever!   Won't you, Josh?   I've seen such nice pretty calico at the store to-day, and I can make up one or two home dresses, like Jane's, only better fitting, of course. In fact, I asked them to send the roll up here to-morrow for you to see."

Mr. Rylands felt relieved. Perhaps his views had changed about the moral effect of her retaining these symbols of her past, for he consented to the calico dresses, not, however, without an inward suspicion that she would not look so well in them, and that the one she had on was more becoming.

Meantime she tried another piece of music. It was equally incongruous and slightly Bacchantic.

"There used to be a mighty pretty dance went to that," she said, nodding her head in time with the music, and assisting the heavily spasmodic attempts of the instrument with the pleasant levity of her voice. " I used to do it."

" Ye might try it now, Ellen," suggested her husband, with a half-frightened, half-amused tolerance.

" *You* play, then," said Mrs. Rylands quickly, offering her seat to him.

Mr. Rylands sat down to the harmonium,

as Mrs. Rylands briskly moved the table and chairs against the wall. Mr. Rylands played slowly and strenuously, as from a conscientious regard of the instrument. Mrs. Rylands stood in the centre of the floor, making a rather pretty, animated picture, as she again stimulated the heavy harmonium swell not only with her voice but her hands and feet. Presently she began to skip.

I should warn the reader here that this was before the " shawl " or " skirt " dancing was in vogue, and I am afraid that pretty Mrs. Rylands's performances would now be voted slow. Her silk skirt and frilled petticoat were lifted just over her small ankles and tiny bronze-kid shoes. In the course of a *pirouette* or two, there was a slight further revelation of blue silk stockings and some delicate embroidery, but really nothing more than may be seen in the sweep of a modern waltz. Suddenly the music ceased. Mr. Rylands had left the harmonium and walked over to the hearth. Mrs. Rylands stopped, and came towards him with a flushed, anxious face.

" It don't seem to go right, does it ? " she

said, with her nervous laugh. " I suppose
I 'm getting too old now, and I don't quite
remember it."

" Better forget it altogether," he replied
gravely. He stopped at seeing a singular
change in her face, and added awkwardly,
" When I told you I did n't want you to be
ashamed of your past, nor to try to forget
what you were, I did n't mean such things
as that ! "

" What did you mean ? " she said timidly.

The truth was that Mr. Rylands did not
know. He had known this sort of thing only
in the abstract. He had never had the least
acquaintance with the class to which his
wife had belonged, nor known anything of
their methods. It was a revelation to him
now, in the woman he loved, and who was
his wife. He was not shocked so much as
he was frightened.

" You shall have the dress to-morrow,
Ellen," he said gently, " and you can put
away these gewgaws. You don't need to
look like Tinkie Clifford."

He did not see the look of triumph that
lit up her eye, but added, " Go on and
play."

She sat down obediently to the instrument. He watched her for a few moments from the toe of her kid slipper on the pedals to the swell of her shoulders above the keyboard, with a strange, abstracted face. Presently she stopped and came over to him.

"And when I 've got these nice calico frocks, and you can't tell me from Jane, and I 'm a good housekeeper, and settle down to be a farmer's wife, maybe I 'll have a secret to tell you."

"A secret?" he repeated gravely. "Why not now?"

Her face was quite aglow with excitement and a certain timid mischief as she laughed: "Not while you are so solemn. It can wait."

He looked at his watch. "I must give some orders to Jim about the stock before he turns in," he said.

"He's gone to the stables already," said Mrs. Rylands.

"No matter; I can go there and find him."

"Shall I bring your boots?" she said quickly.

"I 'll put them on when I pass through

the kitchen. I won't be long away. Now go to bed. You are looking tired," he said gently, as he gazed at the drawn lines about her eyes and mouth. Her former pretty color struck him also as having changed of late, and as being irregular and inharmonious.

As Mrs. Rylands obediently ascended the stairs she heaved a faint sigh, her only recognition of her husband's criticism. He turned and passed quickly into the kitchen. He wanted to be alone to collect his thoughts. But he was surprised to find Jane still there, sitting bolt upright in a chair in the corner. Apparently she had been expecting him, for as he entered she stood up, and wiped her cheek and mouth with one hand, as if to compress her lips the more tightly.

"I reckoned," she began, "that unless you war for forgettin' everythin' in these yer goings on, ye'd be passin' through here to tend to your stock. I've got a word to say to ye, Mr. Rylands. When I first kem over here to help, I got word from the folks around that your wife afore you married her was just one o' them bally dancers. Well,

that was *your* lookout, not mine! Jane
Mackinnon ain't the kind to take everybody's sayin' as gospil, but she kalkilates
to treat folks ez she finds 'em. When she
finds 'em lyin' and deceivin'; when she finds
'em purtendin' one thing and doin' another;
when she finds 'em makin' fools tumble to
'em; playing soots on their own husbands,
and turnin' an honest house into a music-
hall and a fandango shop, she kicks! You
hear me! Jane Mackinnon kicks!"

"What do you mean?" said Mr. Rylands sternly.

"I mean," said Miss Mackinnon, striking
her hips with the back of her hands smartly,
and accenting each word that dropped like
a bullet from her mouth with an additional
blow, — "I — mean — that — your — wife
— had — one — of — her — old — hang-
ers-on — from — 'Frisco — here — in — this
— very — kitchen — all — the — arternoon;
there! I mean that whiles she was waitin'
here for you, she was canoodlin' and cryin'
over old times with him! I saw her myself
through the winder. That's what I mean,
Mr. Joshua Rylands."

"It's false! She had some poor stranger

here with a lame horse. She told me so
herself. "

Jane Mackinnon laughed shrilly.

"Did she tell you that the poor stranger
was young and pretty-faced, with black
moustarches? that his store clothes must
have cost a fortin, saying nothing of his
gold-lined, broadcloth sarrapper? Did she
say that his horse was *so* lame that when I
went to get another' he would n't *wait* for
it? Did she tell you *who* he was?"

"No, she did not know," said Rylands
sternly, but with a whitening face.

"Well, I 'll tell you! The gambler, the
shooter! — the man whose name is black
enough to stain any woman he knows. Jim
recognized him like a shot; he sez, the
moment he clapped eyes on him at the door,
'Dod blasted, if it ain't Jack Hamlin!'"

Little as Mr. Rylands knew of the world,
he had heard that name. But it was not
that he was thinking of. He was thinking
of the camp-fire in the wood, the handsome
figure before it, the tethered horse. He was
thinking of the lighted sitting-room, the fire,
his wife's bare shoulders, her slippers, stockings, and the dance. He saw it all, — a

lightning-flash to his dull imagination. The room seemed to expand and then grow smaller, the figure of Jane to sway backwards and forwards before him. He murmured the name of God with lips that were voiceless, caught at the kitchen table to steady himself, held it till he felt his arms grow rigid, and then recovered himself, — white, cold, and sane.

"Speak a word of this to *her*," he said deliberately, "enter her room while I'm gone, even leave the kitchen before I come back, and I'll throw you into the road. Tell that hired man, if he dares to breathe it to a soul I'll strangle him."

The unlooked-for rage of this quiet, God-fearing man, and dupe, as she believed, was terrible, but convincing. She shrank back into the corner as he coolly drew on his boots and waterproof, and without another word left the house.

He knew what he was going to do as well as if it had been ordained for him. He knew he would find the young man in the wood; for whatever were the truth of the other stories, he and the visitor were identical; he had seen him with his own eyes.

He would confront him face to face and
know all; and until then, he could not see
his wife again. He walked on rapidly, but
without feverishness or mental confusion.
He saw his duty plainly, — if Ellen had
" backslidden," he must give her another
trial. These were his articles of faith. He
should not put her away; but she should
nevermore be wife to him. It was *he* who
had tempted her, it was true; perhaps God
would forgive her for that reason, but *he*
could never love her again.

The fury of the storm had somewhat
abated as he reached the wood. The fire
was still there, but no longer a leaping
flame. A dull glow in the darkness of the
forest aisles was all that indicated its position. Rylands at once plunged in that
direction; he was near enough to see the
red embers when he heard a sharp click,
and a voice called: —

" Hold up! "

Mr. Hamlin was a light sleeper. The
crackle of underbrush had been enough to
disturb him. The voice was his; the click
was the cocking of his revolver.

Rylands was no coward, but halted diplo-
matically.

"Now, then," said Mr. Hamlin's voice, "a little more this way, *in the light*, if you please!"

Rylands moved as directed, and saw Mr. Hamlin lying before the fire, resting easily on one hand, with his revolver in the other.

"Thank you!" said Jack. "Excuse my precautions, but it is night, and this is, for the present, my bedroom."

"My name is Rylands; you called at my house this afternoon and saw my wife," said Rylands slowly.

"I did," said Hamlin. "It was mighty kind of you to return my call so soon, but I did n't expect it."

"I reckon not. But I know who you are, and that you are an old associate of hers, in the days of her sin and unregeneration. I want you to answer me, before God and man, what was your purpose in coming there to-day?"

"Look here! I don't think it 's necessary to drag in strangers to hear my answer," said Jack, lying down again, "but I came to borrow a horse."

"Is that the truth?"

Jack got upon his feet very solemnly, put

on his hat, drew down his waistcoat, and
approached Mr. Rylands with his hands in
his pockets.

" Mr. Rylands," he said, with great suavity of manner, " this is the second time to-
day that I have had the honor of having my
word doubted by your family. Your wife
was good enough to question my assertion
that I did n't know that she was living here,
but that was a woman's vanity. You have
no such excuse. There is my horse yonder,
lame, as you may see. I did n't lame him
for the sake of seeing your wife nor you."

There was that in Mr. Hamlin's audacity
and perfect self-possession which, even while
it irritated, never suggested deceit. He was
too reckless of consequence to lie. Mr.
Rylands was staggered and half convinced.
Nevertheless, he hesitated.

" Dare you tell me everything that happened between my wife and you ? "

" Dare you listen ? " said Mr. Hamlin
quietly.

Mr. Rylands turned a little white. After
a moment he said : —

" Yes."

" Good ! " said Mr. Hamlin. " I like

your grit, though I don't mind telling you
it's the *only* thing I like about you. Sit
down. Well, I haven't seen Nell Montgomery for three years until I met her as
your wife, at your house. She was surprised
as I was, and frightened as I wasn't. She
spent the whole interview in telling me the
history of her marriage and her life with
you, and nothing more. I cannot say that
it was remarkably entertaining, or that she
was as amusing as your wife as she was as
Nell Montgomery, the variety actress. When
she had finished, I came away."

Mr. Rylands, who had seated himself,
made a movement as if to rise. But Mr.
Hamlin laid his hand on his knee.

"I asked you if you dared to listen. I
have something myself to say of that interview. I found your wife wearing the old
dresses that other men had given her, and
she said she wore them because she thought
it pleased you. I found that you, who are
questioning my calling upon her, had already
got the worst of her old chums to visit her
without asking her consent; I found that
instead of being the first one to lie for her
and hide her, you were the first one to tell

anybody her history, just because you thought
it was to the glory of God generally, and
of Joshua Rylands in particular."

"A man's motives are his own," stammered Rylands.

"Sorry you did n't see it when you questioned mine just now," said Jack coolly.

"Then she complained to you?" said
Rylands hesitatingly.

"I did n't say that," said Jack shortly.

"But you found her unhappy?"

"Damnably."

"And you advised her" — said Rylands
tentatively.

"I advised her to chuck you and try
to get a better husband." He paused, and
then added, with a disgusted laugh, "but
she did n't tumble to it, for a d—d silly
reason."

"What reason?" said Rylands hurriedly.

"Said she *loved* you," returned Jack,
kicking a brand back into the fire. Mr.
Rylands's white cheeks flamed out suddenly
like the brand. Seeing which, Jack turned
upon him deliberately.

"Mr. Joshua Rylands, I 've seen many
fools in my time. I 've seen men holding

four aces backed down because they thought
they *knew* the other man had a royal flush!
I've seen a man sell his claim for a wild-cat
share, with the gold lying a foot below him
in the ground he walked on. I've seen a
dead shot shoot wild because he *thought* he
saw something in the other man's eye. I've
seen a heap of God-forsaken fools, but I
never saw one before who claimed Hod as
a pal. You've got a wife a d—d sight
truer to you for what you call her 'sin,'
than you've ever been to her, with all your
d—d salvation! And as you could n't make
her otherwise, though you've tried to hard
enough, it seems to me that for square down-
right chuckle-headedness, you can take the
cake! Good-night! Now, run away and
play! You're making me tired."

"One moment," said Mr. Rylands awkwardly and hurriedly. "I may have wronged
you; I was mistaken. Won't you come back
with me and accept my — our — hospitality?"

"Not much," said Jack. "I left your
house because I thought it better for you
and her that no one should know of my
being there."

"But you were already recognized," said Mr. Rylands. "It was Jane who lied about you, and your return with me will confute her slanders."

"Who?" asked Jack.

"Jane, our hired girl."

Mr. Hamlin uttered an indescribable laugh.

"That's just as well! You simply tell Jane you *saw* me; that I was greatly shocked at what she said, but that I forgive her. I don't think she'll say any more."

Strange to add, Mr. Hamlin's surmise was correct. Mr. Rylands found Jane still in the kitchen alone, terrified, remorseful, yet ever after silent on the subject. Stranger still, the hired man became equally uncommunicative. Mrs. Rylands, attributing her husband's absence only to care of the stock, had gone to bed in a feverish condition, and Mr. Rylands did not deem it prudent to tell her of his interview. The next day she sent for the doctor, and it was deemed necessary for her to keep her bed for a few days. Her husband was singularly attentive and considerate during that time, and it was probable that Mrs. Rylands seized that opportunity to tell him the secret she spoke of the night before. Whatever it was, — for it was not generally known for a few months later, — it seemed to draw them closer together, imparted a protecting dignity to Joshua Rylands, which took the place of his former selfish austerity, gave them a future to talk of confidentially, hopefully, and sometimes foolishly, which took the place of their more foolish past, and when the roll of calico came from the cross roads, it contained also a quantity of fine linen, laces, small caps, and other trifles, somewhat in contrast to the more homely materials ordered.

And when three months were past, the sitting-room was often lit up and made cheerful, particularly on that supreme occasion when, with a great deal of enthusiasm, all the women of the countryside flocked to see Mrs. Rylands and her first baby. And a more considerate and devoted couple than the father and mother they had never known.

THE MAN AT THE SEMAPHORE

In the early days of the Californian immi-
gration, on the extremest point of the sandy
peninsula, where the bay of San Francisco
debouches into the Pacific, there stood a
semaphore telegraph. Tossing its black
arms against the sky, — with its back to the
Golden Gate and that vast expanse of sea
whose nearest shore was Japan, — it signi-
fied to another semaphore further inland the
" rigs " of incoming vessels, by certain uncouth signs, which were again passed on to
Telegraph Hill, San Francisco, where they
reappeared on a third semaphore, and read
to the initiated " schooner," " brig " " ship,"
or " steamer." But all homesick San Francisco had learned the last sign, and on certain days of the month every eye was turned
to welcome those gaunt arms widely extended
at right angles, which meant " sidewheel
steamer " (the only steamer which carried
the mails) and " letters from home." In
the joyful reception accorded to that herald

of glad tidings, very few thought of the
lonely watcher on the sand dunes who dispatched them, or even knew of that desolate station.

For desolate it was beyond description.
The Presidio, with its voiceless, dismounted
cannon and empty embrasures hidden in a
hollow, and the Mission Dolores, with its
crumbling walls and belfry tower lost in
another, made the *ultima thule* of all San
Francisco wandering.   The Cliff House and
Fort Point did not then exist; from Black
Point the curving line of shore of " Yerba
Buena " — or San Francisco — showed only
a stretch of glittering wind-swept sand
dunes, interspersed with straggling gullies
of half-buried black " scrub oak."   The
long six months ' summer sun fiercely beat
upon it from the cloudless sky above; the
long six months' trade winds fiercely beat
upon it from the west ; the monotonous roll-
call of the long Pacific surges regularly beat
upon it from the sea.   Almost impossible
to face by day through sliding sands and
buffeting winds, at night it was impracti-
cable through the dense sea-fog that stole
softly through the Golden Gate at sunset.

Thence, until morning, sea and shore were a trackless waste, bounded only by the warning thunders of the unseen sea. The station itself, a rudely built cabin, with two windows, — one furnished with a telescope, — looked like a heap of driftwood, or a stranded wreck left by the retiring sea; the semaphore — the only object for leagues — lifted above the undulating dunes, took upon itself various shapes, more or less gloomy, according to the hour or weather, — a blasted tree, the masts and clinging spars of a beached ship, a dismantled gallows; or, with the background of a golden sunset across the Gate, and its arms extended at right angles, to a more hopeful fancy it might have seemed the missionary Cross, which the enthusiast Portala lifted on that heathen shore a hundred years before.

Not that Dick Jarman — the solitary station keeper — ever indulged this fancy. An escaped convict from one of her Britannic Majesty's penal colonies, a "stowaway" in the hold of an Australian ship, he had landed penniless in San Francisco, fearful of contact with his more honest countrymen already there, and liable to detection at any

moment. Luckily for him, the English im-
migration consisted mainly of gold-seekers
en route to Sacramento and the southern
mines. He was prudent enough to resist
the temptation to follow them, and accepted
the post of semaphore keeper, — the first
work offered him, — which the meanest im-
migrant, filled with dreams of gold, would
have scorned. His employers asked him no
questions, and demanded no references;
his post could be scarcely deemed one of
trust, — there was no property for him to
abscond with but the telescope; he was removed from temptation and evil company in
his lonely waste; his duties were as mechanical as the instrument he worked, and interruption of them would be instantly known
at San Francisco. For this he would receive
his board and lodging and seventy-five dollars a month, — a sum to be ridiculed in
those " flush days," but which seemed to the
broken-spirited and half-famished stowaway
a princely independence.

And then there was rest and security!
He was free from that torturing anxiety
and fear of detection which had haunted
him night and day for three months. The

ceaseless vigilance and watchful dread he had known since his escape, he could lay aside now. The rude cabin on the sand dune was to him as the long-sought cave to some hunted animal. It seemed impossible that any one would seek him there. He was spared alike the contact of his enemies or the shame of recognizing even a friendly face, until by each he would be forgotten. From his coign of vantage on that desolate waste, and with the aid of his telescope, no stranger could approach within two or three miles of his cabin without undergoing his scrutiny. And at the worst, if he was pursued here, before him was the trackless shore and the boundless sea!

And at times there was a certain satisfaction in watching, unseen and in perfect security, the decks of passing ships. With the aid of his glass he could mingle again with the world from which he was debarred, and gloomily wonder who among those passengers knew their solitary watcher, or had heard of his deeds; it might have made him gloomier had he known that in those eager faces turned towards the golden haven there was little thought of anything but them-

selves. He tried to read in faces on board
the few outgoing ships the record of their
success with a strange envy. They were
returning home! *Home!* For sometimes
— but seldom — he thought of his own
home and his past. It was a miserable past
of forgery and embezzlement that had cul-
minated a career of youthful dissipation and
self-indulgence, and shut him out, forever,
from the staid old English cathedral town
where he was born. He knew that his relations believed and wished him dead. He
thought of this past with little pleasure, but
with little remorse. Like most of his stamp,
he believed it was ill-luck, chance, somebody
else's fault, but never his own responsible
action. He would not repent; he would be
wiser only. And he would not be retaken
— alive!

Two or three months passed in this monotonous duty, in which he partly recovered his
strength and his nerves. He lost his furtive,
restless, watchful look; the bracing sea air
and the burning sun put into his face the
healthy tan and the uplifted frankness of a
sailor. His eyes grew keener from long scan-
ning of the horizon ; he knew where to look

for sails, from the creeping coastwise schooner to the far-rounding merchantman from Cape Horn. He knew the faint line of haze that indicated the steamer long before her masts and funnels became visible. He saw no soul except the solitary boatman of the little " plunger," who landed his weekly provisions at a small cove hard by. The boatman thought his secretiveness and reticence only the surliness of his nation, and cared little for a man who never asked for the news, and to whom he brought no letters. The long nights which wrapped the cabin in sea-fog, and at first seemed to heighten the exile's sense of security, by degrees, however, became monotonous, and incited an odd restlessness, which he was wont to oppose by whiskey, — allowed as a part of his stores, — which, while it dulled his sensibilities, he, however, never permitted to interfere with his mechanical duties.

He had been there five months, and the hills on the opposite shore between Tamalpais were already beginning to show their russet yellow sides. One bright morning he was watching the little fleet of Italian fishing-boats hovering in the bay. This was always

a picturesque spectacle, perhaps the only
one that relieved the general monotony of
his outlook. The quaint lateen sails of dull
red, or yellow, showing against the sparkling
waters, and the red caps or handkerchiefs
of the fishermen, might have attracted even
a more abstracted man. Suddenly one of
the larger boats tacked, and made directly
for the little cove where his weekly plunger
used to land. In an instant he was alert
and suspicious. But a close examination of
the boat through his glass satisfied him that
it contained, in addition to the crew, only
two or three women, apparently the family
of the fishermen. As it ran up on the
beach and the entire party disembarked, he
could see it was merely a careless, peaceable
invasion, and he thought no more about it.
The strangers wandered about the sands,
gesticulating and laughing; they brought
a pot ashore, built a fire, and cooked a
homely meal. He could see that from time
to time the semaphore — evidently a novelty to them — had attracted their attention; and having occasion to signal the
arrival of a bark, the working of the uncouth arms of the instrument drew the chil-

dren in half-frightened curiosity towards it, although the others held aloof, as if fearful of trespassing upon some work of the government, no doubt secretly guarded by the police. A few mornings later he was surprised to see upon the beach, near the same locality, a small heap of lumber which had evidently been landed in the early morning fog. The next day an old tent appeared on the spot, and the men, evidently fishermen, began the erection of a rude cabin beside it. Jarman had been long enough there to know that it was government land, and that these manifestly humble " squatters " upon it would not be interfered with for some time to come. He began to be uneasy again ; it was true they were fully half a mile from him, and they were foreigners ; but might not their reckless invasion of the law attract others, in this lawless country, to do the same ? It ought to be stopped. For once Richard Jarman sided with legal authority.

But when the cabin was completed, it was evident from what he saw of its rude structure that it was only a temporary shelter for the fisherman's family and the stores, and refitting of the fishing-boat, more convenient to them than the San Francisco wharves. The beach was utilized for the mending of nets and sails, and thus became half picturesque. In spite of the keen northwestern trades, the cloudless, sunshiny mornings tempted these southerners back to their native *al fresco* existence; they not only basked in the sun, but many of their household duties, and even the mysteries of their toilet, were performed in the open air. They did not seem to care to penetrate into the desolate region behind them; their half-amphibious habit kept them near the water's edge, and Richard Jarman, after taking his limited walks for the first few mornings in another direction, found it no longer necessary to avoid the locality, and even forgot their propinquity.

But one morning, as the fog was clearing away and the sparkle of the distant sea was beginning to show from his window, he rose from his belated breakfast to fetch water from the " breaker " outside, which had to be replenished weekly from Sancelito, as there was no spring in his vicinity. As he opened the door, he was inexpressibly startled by the figure of a young woman standing in front of it, who, however, half fearfully, half laughingly withdrew before him. But his own manifest disturbance apparently gave her courage.

" I jess was looking at that thing," she said bashfully, pointing to the semaphore.

He was still more astonished, for, looking at her dark eyes and olive complexion, he had expected her to speak Italian or broken English. And, possibly because for a long time he had seen and known little of women, he was quite struck with her good looks. He hesitated, stammered, and then said : —

" Won't you come in ? "

She drew back still farther and made a rapid gesture of negation with her head, her hand, and even her whole lithe figure. Then she said, with a decided American intonation : —

" No, sir."

" Why not ? " said Jarman mechanically.

The girl sidled up against the cabin, keeping her eyes fixed on Jarman with a certain youthful shrewdness.

" Oh, you know ! " she said.

" I really do not. Tell me why."

She drew herself up against the wall a little proudly, though still youthfully, with her hands behind her.

" I ain't that kind of girl," she said simply.

The blood rushed to Jarman's cheeks. Dissipated and abandoned as his life had been, small respecter of women as he was, he was shocked and shamed. Knowing too, as he did, how absorbed he was in other things, he was indignant, because not guilty.

" Do as you please, then," he said shortly, and reëntered the cabin. But the next moment he saw his error in betraying an irritation that was open to misconstruction. He came out again, scarcely looking at the girl, who was lounging away.

" Do you want me to explain to you how the thing works? " he said indifferently. " I can't show you unless a ship comes in."

The girl's eyes brightened softly as she turned to him.

" Do tell me," she said, with an anticipatory smile and flash of white teeth. " Won't you? "

She certainly was very pretty and simple, in spite of her late speech. Jarman briefly

explained to her the movements of the semaphore arms and their different significance.
She listened with her capped head a little
on one side like an attentive bird, and her
arms unconsciously imitating the signs.
Certainly, for all that she *spoke* like an
American, her gesticulation was Italian.

" And then," she said triumphantly when
he paused, " when the sailors see that sign
up they know they are coming in the harbor."

Jarman smiled, as he had not smiled
since he had been there. He corrected this
mistake of her eager haste to show her intelligence, and, taking the telescope, pointed
out the other semaphore, — a thin black
outline on a distant inland hill. He then
explained how *his* signs were repeated by
that instrument to San Francisco.

"My! Why, I always allowed that was
only the cross stuck up in the Lone Mountain Cemetery," she said.

" You are a Catholic ? "

" I reckon."

" And you are an Italian ? "

" Father is, but mother was a 'Merikan,
same as me. Mother 's dead."

"And your father is the fisherman yonder?"

"Yes, — but," with a look of pride, "he's got the biggest boat of any."

"And only you and your family are ashore here?"

"Yes, and sometimes Mark." She laughed an odd little laugh.

"Mark? Who's he?" he asked quickly.

He had not noticed the sudden coquettish pose and half-affected bashfulness of the girl; he was thinking only of the possibility of detection by strangers.

"Oh, he is Marco Franti, but I call him 'Mark.' It's the same name, you know, and it makes him mad," said the girl, with the same suggestion of archness and coquetry.

But all this was lost on Jarman.

"Oh, another Italian," he said, relieved. She turned away a little awkwardly when he added, "But you have n t told me *your* name, you know."

"Cara."

"Cara, — that's 'dear' in Italian, is n't it?" he said, with a reminiscence of the opera and a half smile.

" Yes," she said a little scornfully, " but it means Carlotta, — Charlotte, you know. Some girls call me Charley," she said hurriedly.

" I see — Cara — or Carlotta Franti. "

To his surprise she burst into a peal of laughter.

" I reckon not *yet.* Franti is Mark's name, not mine. Mine is Murano, — Carlotta Murano. Good-by." She moved away, then stopped suddenly and said, " I 'm comin' again some time when the thing is working," and with a nod of her head, ran away. He looked after her ; could see the outlines of her youthful figure in her slim cotton gown, — limp and clinging in the damp sea air, and the sudden revelation of her bare ankles thrust stockingless into canvas shoes.

He went back into his cabin, when presently his attention was engrossed by an incoming vessel. He made the signals, half expecting, almost hoping, that the girl would return to watch him. But her figure was already lost in the sand dunes. Yet he fancied he still heard the echoes of her voice and his own in this cabin which had so long been dumb and voiceless, and he now started at every sound. For the first time he became aware of the dreadful disorder and untidiness of its uninvaded privacy. He could scarcely believe he had been living with his stove, his bed, and cooking utensils all in one corner of the barnlike room, and he began to put them "to rights" in a rough, hard formality, strongly suggestive of his convict experience. He rolled up his blankets into a hard cylinder at the head of his cot. He scraped out his kettles and saucepans, and even "washed down" the floor, afterwards sprinkling clean dry sand, hot with the noonday sunshine, on its half-dried boards. In arranging these domestic details he had to change the position of a little mirror; and glancing at it for the first time in many days, he was dissatisfied with his straggling beard, — grown during his voyage from Australia, — and although he had retained it as a disguise, he at once shaved it off, leaving only a mustache, and revealing a face from which a healthier life and out-of-door existence had removed the last traces of vice and dissipation. But he did not know it.

All the next day he thought of his fair visitor, and found himself often repeating her odd remark that she was " not that kind of girl," with a smile that was alternately significant or vacant. Evidently she could take care of herself, he thought, although her very good looks no doubt had exposed her to the rude attentions of fishermen or the common drift of San Francisco wharves. Perhaps this was why her father brought her here. When the day passed and she came not, he began vaguely to wonder if he had been rude to her. Perhaps he had taken her simple remark too seriously; perhaps she had expected he would only laugh, and had found him dull and stupid. Perhaps he had thrown away an opportunity. An opportunity for what? To renew his old life and habits? No, no! The horrors of his recent imprisonment and escape were still too fresh in his memory; he was not safe yet. Then he wondered if he had not grown spiritless and pigeon-livered in his solitude and loneliness. The next day he searched for her with his glass, and saw her playing with one of the children on the beach, — a very picture of child or nymph

like innocence.   Perhaps it was because she
was not "that kind of girl" that she had
attracted him.   He laughed bitterly.   Yes;
that was very funny; he, an escaped convict, drawn towards honest, simple innocence!
Yet he knew — he was positive — he had
not thought of any ill when he spoke to her.
He took a singular, a ridiculous pride in
and credit to himself for that.   He repeated
it incessantly to himself.   Then what made
her angry?   Himself!   The devil!   Did
he carry, then, the record of his past life
forever in his face — in his speech — in his
manners?   The thought made him sullen.
The next day he would not look towards the
shore ; it was wonderful what excitement
and satisfaction he got out of that strange
act of self-denial; it made the day seem full
that had been so vacant before; yet he
could not tell why or wherefore.   He felt
injured, but he rather liked it.   Yet in the
night he was struck with the idea that she
might have gone back to San Francisco,
and he lay awake longing for the morning
light to satisfy him.   Yet when the fog
cleared, and from a nearer point, behind a
sand dune, he discovered, by the aid of his

glass, that she was seated on the sun-warmed sands combing out her long hair like a mermaid, he immediately returned to the cabin, and that morning looked no more that way. In the afternoon, there being no sails in sight, he turned aside from the bay and walked westward towards the ocean, halting only at the league-long line of foam which marked the breaking Pacific surges. Here he was surprised to see a little child, half-naked, following barefooted the creeping line of spume, or running after the detached and quivering scraps of foam that chased each other over the wet sand, and only a little further on, to come upon Cara herself, sitting with her elbows on her knees and her round chin in her hands, apparently gazing over the waste of waters before her. A sudden and inexplicable shyness overtook him. He hesitated, and stepped half-hidden in a gully between the sand dunes.

As yet he had not been observed; the young girl called to the child and, suddenly rising, threw off her red cap and shawl and quietly began to disrobe herself. A couple of coarse towels were at her feet. Jarman instantly comprehended that she was going to bathe with the child. She undoubtedly knew as well as he did that she was safe in that solitude; that no one could intrude upon her privacy from the bay shore, nor from the desolate inland trail to the sea, without her knowledge. Of his own contiguity she had evidently taken no thought, believing him safely housed in his cabin beside the semaphore. She lifted her hands, and with a sudden movement shook out her long hair and let it fall down her back at the same moment that her unloosened blouse began to slip from her shoulders. Richard Jarman turned quickly and walked noiselessly and rapidly away, until the little hillock had shut out the beach.

His retreat was as sudden, unreasoning, and unpremeditated as his intrusion. It was not like himself, he knew, and yet it was as perfectly instinctive and natural as if he had intruded upon a sister. In the South Seas he had seen native girls diving beside the vessels for coins, but they had provoked no such instinct as that which possessed him now. More than that, he swept a quick, wrathful glance along the horizon on either

side, and then, mounting a remote hillock
which still hid him from the beach, he sat
there and kept watch and ward. From time
to time the strong sea-breeze brought him
the sound of infantine screams and shouts of
girlish laughter from the unseen shore ; he
only looked the more keenly and suspiciously
for any wandering trespasser, and did not
turn his head. He lay there nearly half an
hour, and when the sounds had ceased, rose
and made his way slowly back to the cabin.
He had not gone many yards before he
heard the twitter of voices and smothered
laughter behind him. He turned ; it was
Cara and the child, — a girl of six or seven.
Cara's face was rosy, — possibly from her
bath, and possibly from some shame-faced
consciousness. He slackened his pace, and
as they ranged beside him said, " Good-
morning ! "

" Lord ! " said Cara, stifling another
laugh, " we did n't know you were around ;
we thought you were always 'tending your
telegraph, did n't we, Lucy ? " (to the child,
who was convulsed with mirth and sheepish-
ness). " Why, we 've been taking a wash
in the sea." She tried to gather up her

long hair, which had been left to stray over
her shoulders and dry in the sunlight, and
even made a slight pretense of trying to
conceal the wet towels they were carrying.

Jarman did not laugh. " If you had told
me," he said gravely, " I could have kept
watch for you with my glass while you were
there. I could see further than you."

" Tould you see *us?* " asked the little girl,
with hopeful vivacity.

" No ! " said Jarman, with masterly evasion. " There are little sandhills between
this and the beach."

" Then how tould other people see us? "
persisted the child.

Jarman could see that the older girl was
evidently embarrassed, and changed the
subject. " I sometimes go out," he said,
" when I can see there are no vessels in
sight, and I take my glass with me. , I can
always get back in time to make signals. I
thought, in fact," he said, glancing at Cara's
brightening face, " that I might get as far
as your house on the shore some day." To
his surprise, her embarrassment suddenly
seemed to increase, although she had looked
relieved before, and she did not reply.
After a moment she said abruptly : —

" Did you ever see the sea-lions ? "

" No," said Jarman.

" Not the big ones on Seal Rock, beyond the cliffs ? " continued the girl, in real astonishment.

" No," repeated Jarman. " I never walked in that direction." He vaguely remembered that they were a curiosity which sometimes attracted parties thither, and for that reason he had avoided the spot.

" Why, I have sailed all around the rock in father's boat," continued Cara, with importance. " That 's the best way to see 'em, and folks from Frisco sometimes takes a sail out there just on purpose, — it 's too sandy to walk or drive there. But it 's only a step from here. Look here ! " she said suddenly, and frankly opening her fine eyes upon him. " I 'm going to take Lucy there to-morrow, and I 'll show you." Jarman felt his cheeks flush quickly with a pleasure that embarrassed him. " It won't take long," added Cara, mistaking his momentary hesitation, " and you can leave your telegraph alone. Nobody will be there, so no one will see you and nobody know it."

He would have gone then, anyway, he

knew, yet in his absurd self-consciousness he was glad that her last suggestion had relieved him of a sense of reckless compliance. He assented eagerly, when with a wave of her hand, a flash of her white teeth, and the same abruptness she had shown at their last parting, she caught Lucy by the arm and darted away in a romping race to her dwelling. Jarman started after her. He had not wanted to go to her father's house particularly, but why was *she* evidently as averse to it? With the subtle pleasure that this admission gave him there was a faint stirring of suspicion.

It was gone when he found her and Lucy the next morning, radiant with the sunshine, before his door. The restraint of their previous meetings had been removed in some mysterious way, and they chatted gayly as they walked towards the cliffs. She asked him frankly many questions about himself, why he had come there, and if he " was n't lonely; " she answered frankly — I fear much more frankly than he answered her — the many questions he asked her about herself and her friends. When they reached the cliffs they descended to the beach, which they found deserted. Before them — it seemed scarce a pistol shot from the shore — arose a high, broad rock, beaten at its base by the long Pacific surf, on which a number of shapeless animals were uncouthly disporting. This was Seal Rock, the goal of their journey.

Yet after a few moments they no longer looked at it, but seated on the sand, with Lucy gathering shells at the water's edge, they continued their talk. Presently the talk became eager confidences, and then, — there were long and dangerous lapses of silence, when both were fain to make perfunctory talk with Lucy on the beach. After one of those silences Jarman said : —

" Do you know I rather thought yesterday you did n't want me to come to your father's house. Why was that ? "

" Because Marco was there," said the girl frankly.

" What had *he* to do with it ? " said Jarman abruptly.

" He wants to marry me."

" And do you want to marry *him ?* " said Jarman quickly.

" No," said the girl passionately.

" Why don't you get rid of him, then ? "

" I can't, he 's hiding here, — he 's father's friend."

" Hiding ?   What 's he been doing ? "

" Stealing.   Stealing gold-dust from miners.   I never cared for him anyway.   And I hate a thief ! "

She looked up quickly.   Jarman had risen to his feet, his face turned to sea.

" What are you looking at ? " she said wonderingly.

" A ship," said Jarman, in a strange, hoarse voice.   " I must hurry back and signal.   I 'm afraid I have n't even time to walk with you, — I must run for it.   Goodby ! "

He turned without offering his hand and ran hurriedly in the direction of the semaphore.

Cara, discomfited, turned her black eyes to the sea.   But it seemed empty as before, no sail, no ship on the horizon line, only a little schooner slowly beating out of the Gate.   Ah, well !   It no doubt was there, — that sail, — though she could not see it ; how keen and far-seeing his handsome, honest eyes were !   She heaved a little sigh, and, calling Lucy to her side, began to make her way homeward. But she kept her eyes on the semaphore; it seemed to her the next thing to seeing him, — this man she was beginning to love. She waited for the gaunt arms to move with the signal of the vessel he had seen. But, strange to say, it was motionless. He must have been mistaken.

All this, however, was driven from her mind in the excitement that she found on her return thrilling her own family. They had been warned that a police boat with detectives on board had been dispatched from San Francisco to the cove. Luckily, they had managed to convey the fugitive Franti on board a coastwise schooner, — Cara started as she remembered the one she had seen beating out of the Gate, — and he was now safe from pursuit. Cara felt relieved; at the same time she felt a strange joy at her heart, which sent the conscious blood to her cheek. She was not thinking of the escaped Marco, but of Jarman. Later, when the police boat arrived, — whether the detectives had been forewarned of Marco's escape or not, — they contented themselves with a formal search of the little fishing-hut and departed. But their boat remained lying off the shore.

That night Cara tossed sleeplessly on her bed ; she was sorry she had ever spoken of Marco to Jarman. It was unnecessary now ; perhaps he disbelieved her and thought she loved Marco ; perhaps that was the reason of his strange and abrupt leave-taking that afternoon. She longed for the next day, she could tell him everything now.

Towards morning she slept fitfully, but was awakened by the sound of voices on the sands outside the hut. Its flimsy structure, already warped by the fierce day-long sun, allowed her through chinks and crevices not only to recognize the voices of the detectives, but to hear distinctly what they said. Suddenly the name of Jarman struck upon her ear. She sat upright in bed, breathless.

" Are you sure it's the same man ? " asked a second voice.

" Perfectly," answered the first. " He was tracked to 'Frisco, but disappeared the day he landed. We knew from our agents that he never left the bay. And when we found that somebody answering his description got the post of telegraph operator out here, we knew that we had spotted our man and the £250 sterling offered for his capture."

" But that was five months ago. Why did n't you take him then ? "

" Could n't ! For we could n't hold him without the extradition papers from Australia. We sent for 'em ; they 're due to-day or to-morrow on the mail steamer."

" But he might have got away at any time ? "

" He could n't without our knowing it. Don't you see ? Every time the signals went up, we in San Francisco knew he was at his post. We had him safe, out here on these sandhills, as if he 'd been under lock and key in 'Frisco. He was his own keeper, and reported to us."

" But since you 're here and expect the papers to-morrow, why don't you ' cop ' him now ? "

" Because there is n't a judge in San Francisco that would hold him a moment unless he had those extradition papers before him. He 'd be discharged, and escape."

" Then what are you going to do ? "

" As soon as the steamer is signaled in
'Frisco, we'll board her in the bay, get the
papers, and drop down upon him."

" I see ; and as *he's* the signal man, the
darned fool " —

" Will give the signal himself."

The laugh that followed was so cruel that
the young girl shuddered. But the next
moment she slipped from the bed, erect,
pale, and determined.

The voices seemed gradually to retreat.
She dressed herself hurriedly, and passed
noiselessly through the room of her still
sleeping parent, and passed out. A gray
fog was lifting slowly over the sands and
sea, and the police boat was gone. She no
longer hesitated, but ran quickly in the direction of Jarman's cabin. As she ran, her
mind seemed to be swept clear of all illusion
and fancy ; she saw plainly everything that
had happened ; she knew the mystery of
Jarman's presence here, — the secret of his
life, — the dreadful cruelty of her remark
to him, — the man that she knew now she
loved. The sun was painting the black arms
of the semaphore as she toiled over the last

stretch of sand and knocked loudly at the
door. There was no reply. She knocked
again; the cabin was silent. Had he already fled? — and without seeing her and
knowing all! She tried the handle of the
door; it yielded; she stepped boldly into
the room, with his name upon her lips. He
was lying fully dressed upon his couch.
She ran eagerly to his side and stopped.
It needed only a single glance at his con-
gested face, his lips parted with his heavy
breath, to see that the man was hopelessly,
helplessly drunk!

Yet even then, without knowing that it
was her thoughtless speech which had driven
him to seek this foolish oblivion of remorse
and sorrow, she saw only his *helplessness*.
She tried in vain to rouse him; he only
muttered a few incoherent words and sank
back again. She looked despairingly around.
Something must be done; the steamer might
be visible at any moment. Ah, yes, — the
telescope! She seized it and swept the
horizon. There was a faint streak of haze
against the line of sea and sky, abreast the
Golden Gate. He had once told her what
it meant. It *was* the steamer! A sudden

thought leaped into her clear and active brain. If the police boat should chance to see that haze too, and saw no warning signal from the semaphore, they would suspect something. That signal must be made, *but not the right one !* She remembered quickly how he had explained to her the difference between the signals for a coasting steamer and the one that brought the mails. At that distance the police boat could not detect whether the semaphore's arms were extended to perfect right angles for the mail steamer, or if the left arm slightly deflected for a coasting steamer. She ran out to the windlass and seized the crank. For a moment it defied her strength ; she redoubled her efforts : it began to creak and groan, the great arms were slowly uplifted, and the signal made.

But the familiar sounds of the moving machinery had pierced through Jarman's sluggish consciousness as no other sound in heaven or earth could have done, and awakened him to the one dominant sense he had left, — the habit of duty. She heard him roll from the bed with an oath, stumble to the door, and saw him dash forward with an affrighted face, and plunge his head into a bucket of water. He emerged from it pale and dripping, but with the full light of reason and consciousness in his eyes. He started when he saw her; even then she would have fled, but he caught her firmly by the wrist.

Then with a hurried, trembling voice she told him all and everything. He listened in silence, and only at the end raised her hand gravely to his lips.

"And now," she added tremulously, "you must fly — quick — at once; or it will be too late ! "

But Richard Jarman walked slowly to the door of his cabin, still holding her hand, and said quietly, pointing to his only chair: —

" Sit down; we must talk first."

What they said was never known, but a few moments later they left the cabin, Jarman carrying in a small bag all his possessions, and Cara leaning on his arm. An hour later the priest of the Mission Dolores was called upon to unite in matrimony a frank, honest-looking sailor and an Italian gypsy-looking girl. There were many hasty unions in those days, and the Holy Church was only too glad to be able to give them its legal indorsement. But the good Padre was a little sorry for the honest sailor, and gave the girl some serious advice.

The San Francisco papers the next morning threw some dubious light upon the matter in a paragraph headed, " Another Police Fiasco."

" We understand that the indefatigable police of San Francisco, after ascertaining that Marco Franti, the noted gold-dust thief, was hiding on the shore near the Presidio, proceeded there with great solemnity, and arrived, as usual, a few hours after their man had escaped. But the climax of incapacity was reached when, as it is alleged, the sweetheart of the absconding Franti, and daughter of a brother fisherman, eloped still later, and joined her lover under the very noses of the police. The attempt of the detectives to excuse themselves at headquarters by reporting that they were also on the track of an alleged escaped Sydney Duck was received with the derision and skepticism it deserved, as it seemed that these worthies mistook the mail steamer, which they should have boarded to get certain extradition papers, for a coasting steamer."

.   .   .   .

It was not until four years later that Murano was delighted to recognize in the husband of his long-lost daughter a very rich cattle-owner in Southern California, called Jarman; but he never knew that he had been an escaped convict from Sydney, who had lately received a full pardon through the instrumentality of divers distinguished people in Australia.

AN ESMERALDA OF ROCKY CAÑON

It is to be feared that the hero of this chronicle began life as an impostor. He was offered to the credulous and sympathetic family of a San Francisco citizen as a lamb, who, unless bought as a playmate for the children, would inevitably pass into the butcher's hands. A combination of refined sensibility and urban ignorance of nature prevented them from discerning certain glaring facts that betrayed his caprid origin. So a ribbon was duly tied round his neck, and in pleasing emulation of the legendary "Mary," he was taken to school by the confiding children. Here, alas! the fraud was discovered, and history was reversed by his being turned out by the teacher, because he was *not* "a lamb at school." Nevertheless, the kind-hearted mother of the family persisted in retaining him, on the plea that he might yet become "useful." To her husband's feeble sugges-

tion of " gloves," she returned a scornful
negative, and spoke of the weakly infant of
a neighbor, who might later receive nourishment from this providential animal. But
even this hope was destroyed by the eventual
discovery of his sex. Nothing remained
now but to accept him as an ordinary kid,
and to find amusement in his accomplish-
ments, — eating, climbing, and butting. It
must be confessed that these were of a superior quality; a capacity to eat everything
from a cambric handkerchief to an election
poster, an agility which brought him even to
the roofs of houses, and a power of overturn-
ing by a single push the chubbiest child who
opposed him, made him a fearful joy to the
nursery. This last quality was incautiously
developed in him by a negro boy-servant,
who, later, was hurriedly propelled down a
flight of stairs by his too proficient scholar.
Having once tasted victory, " Billy " needed
no further incitement to his performances.
The small wagon which he sometimes consented to draw for the benefit of the children
never hindered his attempts to butt the
passer-by. On the contrary, on well-known
scientific principles he added the impact of

the bodies of the children projected over his head in his charge, and the infelicitous pedestrian found himself not only knocked off his legs by Billy, but bombarded by the whole nursery.

Delightful as was this recreation to juvenile limbs, it was felt to be dangerous to the adult public. Indignant protestations were made, and as Billy could not be kept in the house, he may be said to have at last butted himself out of that sympathetic family and into a hard and unfeeling world. One morning he broke his tether in the small back yard. For several days thereafter he displayed himself in guilty freedom on the tops of adjacent walls and outhouses. The San Francisco suburb where his credulous protectors lived was still in a volcanic state of disruption, caused by the grading of new streets through rocks and sandhills. In consequence the roofs of some houses were on the level of the doorsteps of others, and were especially adapted to Billy's performances. One afternoon, to the admiring and perplexed eyes of the nursery, he was discovered standing on the apex of a neighbor's new Elizabethan chim-

ney, on a space scarcely larger than the
crown of a hat, calmly surveying the world
beneath him. High infantile voices appealed
to him in vain; baby arms were outstretched
to him in hopeless invitation; he remained
exalted and obdurate, like Milton's hero,
probably by his own merit "raised to that
bad eminence." Indeed, there was already
something Satanic in his budding horns and
pointed mask as the smoke curled softly
around him. Then he appropriately vanished, and San Francisco knew him no more.
At the same time, however, one Owen
M'Ginnis, a neighboring sandhill squatter,
also disappeared, leaving San Francisco for
the southern mines, and he was said to have
taken Billy with him, — for no conceivable
reason except for companionship. Howbeit,
it was the turning-point of Billy's career;
such restraint as kindness, civilization, or
even policemen had exercised upon his nature was gone. He retained, I fear, a certain wicked intelligence, picked up in San
Francisco with the newspapers and theatri-
cal and election posters he had consumed.
He reappeared at Rocky Cañon among the
miners as an exceedingly agile chamois,

with the low cunning of a satyr. That was all that civilization had done for him!

If Mr. M'Ginnis had fondly conceived that he would make Billy "useful," as well as companionable, he was singularly mis-, taken. Horses and mules were scarce in Rocky Cañon, and he attempted to utilize Billy by making him draw a small cart, laden with auriferous earth, from his claim to the river. Billy, rapidly gaining strength, was quite equal to the task, but alas! not his inborn propensity. An incautious gesture from the first passing miner Billy chose to construe into the usual challenge. Lowering his head, from which his budding horns had been already pruned by his master, he instantly went for his challenger, cart and all. Again the scientific law already pointed out prevailed. With the shock of the onset the entire contents of the cart arose and poured over the astonished miner, burying him from sight. In any other but a Californian mining-camp such a propensity in a draught animal would have been condemned, on account of the damage and suffering it entailed, but in Rocky Cañon it proved unprofitable to the owner from the

very amusement and interest it excited.
Miners lay in wait for Billy with a "green-
horn," or new-comer, whom they would put
up to challenge the animal by some indis-
creet gesture. In this way hardly a cartload
of "pay-gravel" ever arrived safely at its
destination, and the unfortunate M'Ginnis
was compelled to withdraw Billy as a beast
of burden. It was whispered that so great
had his propensity become, under repeated
provocation, that M'Ginnis himself was no
longer safe. Going ahead of his cart one
day to remove a fallen bough from the trail,
Billy construed the act of stooping into a
playful challenge from his master, — with
the inevitable result.

The next day M'Ginnis appeared with a
wheelbarrow, but without Billy. From that
day he was relegated to the rocky crags
above the camp, from whence he was only
lured occasionally by the mischievous miners, who wished to exhibit his peculiar performances. For although Billy had ample
food and sustenance among the crags, he
had still a civilized longing for posters; and
whenever a circus, a concert, or a political
meeting was "billed" in the settlement, he

was on hand while the paste was yet fresh
and succulent.   In this way it was averred
that he once removed a gigantic theatre bill
setting forth the charms of the " Sacramento
Pet," and being caught in the act by the
advance agent, was pursued through the
main street, carrying the damp bill on his
horns, eventually affixing it, after his own
peculiar fashion, on the back of Judge
Boompointer, who was standing in front of
his own court-house.

In connection with the visits of this young
lady another story concerning Billy survives
in the legends of Rocky Cañon.   Colonel
Starbottle was at that time passing through
the settlement on election business, and it
was part of his chivalrous admiration for
the sex to pay a visit to the pretty actress.
The single waiting-room of the little hotel
gave upon the veranda, which was also level
with the street.   After a brief yet gallant
interview, in which he oratorically expressed
the gratitude of the settlement with old-
fashioned Southern courtesy, Colonel Starbottle lifted the chubby little hand of the
" Pet " to his lips, and, with a low bow,
backed out upon the veranda.   But the Pet

was astounded by his instant reappearance, and by his apparently casting himself passionately and hurriedly at her feet! It is needless to say that he was followed closely by Billy, who from the street had casually noticed him, and construed his novel exit into an ungentlemanly challenge.

Billy's visits, however, became less frequent, and as Rocky Cañon underwent the changes incidental to mining settlements, he was presently forgotten in the invasion of a few Southwestern families, and the adoption of amusements less practical and turbulent than he had afforded. It was alleged that he was still seen in the more secluded fastnesses of the mountains, having reverted to a wild state, and it was suggested by one or two of the more adventurous that he might yet become edible, and a fair object of chase. A traveler through the Upper Pass of the cañon related how he had seen a savage-looking, hairy animal like a small elk perched upon inaccessible rocks, but always out of gunshot. But these and other legends were set at naught and overthrown by an unexpected incident.

The Pioneer Coach was toiling up the

long grade towards Skinners Pass when
Yuba Bill suddenly pulled up, with his feet
on the brake.

"Jimminy!" he ejaculated, drawing a
deep breath.

The startled passenger beside him on
the box followed the direction of his eyes.
Through an opening in the wayside pines
he could see, a few hundred yards away, a
cuplike hollow in the hillside of the vividest
green. In the centre a young girl of fifteen
or sixteen was dancing and keeping step to
the castanet "click" of a pair of "bones,"
such as negro minstrels use, held in her
hands above her head. But, more singular
still, a few paces before her a large goat,
with its neck roughly wreathed with flowers
and vines, was taking ungainly bounds and
leaps in imitation of its companion. The
wild background of the Sierras, the pastoral
hollow, the incongruousness of the figures,
and the vivid color of the girl's red flannel
petticoat showing beneath her calico skirt,
that had been pinned around her waist, made
a striking picture, which by this time had attracted all eyes. Perhaps the dancing of the
girl suggested a negro "break-down" rather

than any known sylvan measure; but all
this, and even the clatter of the bones, was
made gracious by the distance.

"Esmeralda! by the living Harry!"
shouted the excited passenger on the box.

Yuba Bill took his feet off the brake, and
turned a look of deep scorn upon his companion as he gathered the reins again.

"It's that blanked goat, outer Rocky
Cañon beyond, and Polly Harkness! How
did she ever come to take up with *him*?"

Nevertheless, as soon as the coach reached
Rocky Cañon, the story was quickly told
by the passengers, corroborated by Yuba
Bill, and highly colored by the observer on
the box-seat. Harkness was known to be a
new-comer who lived with his wife and only
daughter on the other side of Skinners Pass.
He was a "logger" and charcoal-burner,
who had eaten his way into the serried ranks
of pines below the pass, and established
in these efforts an almost insurmountable
cordon of fallen trees, stripped bark, and
charcoal pits around the clearing where his
rude log hut stood, — which kept his seclusion unbroken. He was said to be a half-
savage mountaineer from Georgia, in whose

rude fastnesses he had distilled unlawful whiskey, and that his tastes and habits unfitted
him for civilization. His wife chewed and
smoked; he was believed to make a fiery
brew of his own from acorns and pine nuts;
he seldom came to Rocky Cañon except for
provisions; his logs were slipped down a
"shoot" or slide to the river, where they
voyaged once a month to a distant mill, but
he did not accompany them. The daughter,
seldom seen at Rocky Cañon, was a half-
grown girl, brown as autumn fern, wild-eyed,
disheveled, in a homespun skirt, sunbonnet,
and boy's brogans. Such were the plain
facts which skeptical Rocky Cañon opposed
to the passengers' legends. Nevertheless,
some of the younger miners found it not out
of their way to go over Skinners Pass on
the journey to the river, but with what success was not told. It was said, however,
that a celebrated New York artist, making
a tour of California, was on the coach one
day going through the pass, and preserved
the memory of what he saw there in a well-
known picture entitled "Dancing Nymph
and Satyr," said by competent critics to
be "replete with the study of Greek life."

This did not affect Rocky Cañon, where the study of mythology was presumably displaced by an experience of more wonderful flesh-and-blood people, but later it was remembered with some significance.

Among the improvements already noted, a zinc and wooden chapel had been erected in the main street, where a certain popular revivalist preacher of a peculiar Southwestern sect regularly held exhortatory services. His rude emotional power over his ignorant fellow-sectarians was well known, while curiosity drew others. His effect upon the females of his flock was hysterical and sensational. Women prematurely aged by frontier drudgery and child-bearing, girls who had known only the rigors and pains of a half-equipped, ill-nourished youth in their battling with the hard realities of nature around them, all found a strange fascination in the extravagant glories and privileges of the unseen world he pictured to them, which they might have found in the fairy tales and nursery legends of civilized children, had they known them. Personally he was not attractive ; his thin pointed face, and bushy hair rising on either side of his square forehead in two rounded knots, and his long, straggling, wiry beard dropping from a strong neck and shoulders, were indeed of a common Southwestern type ; yet in him they suggested something more. This was voiced by a miner who attended his first service, and as the Reverend Mr. Withholder rose in the pulpit, the former was heard to audibly ejaculate, "Dod blasted ! — if it ain't Billy ! " But when on the following Sunday, to everybody's astonishment, Polly Harkness, in a new white muslin frock and broad-brimmed Leghorn hat, appeared before the church door with the real Billy, and exchanged conversation with the preacher, the likeness was appalling.

I grieve to say that the goat was at once christened by Rocky Cañon as " The Reverend Billy," and the minister himself was Billy's " brother." More than that, when an attempt was made by outsiders, during the service, to inveigle the tethered goat into his old butting performances, and he took not the least notice of their insults and challenges, the epithet " blanked hypocrite " was added to his title.

Had he really reformed ? Had his pas-

toral life with his nymph-like mistress completely cured him of his pugnacious propensity, or had he simply found it was
inconsistent with his dancing, and seriously
interfered with his "fancy steps"? Had
he found tracts and hymn-books were as
edible as theatre posters? These were questions that Rocky Cañon discussed lightly,
although there was always the more serious
mystery of the relations of the Reverend
Mr. Withholder, Polly Harkness, and the
goat towards each other. The appearance
of Polly at church was no doubt due to the
minister's active canvass of the districts.
But had he ever heard of Polly's dancing
with the goat? And where in this plain,
angular, badly dressed Polly was hidden that
beautiful vision of the dancing nymph which
had enthralled so many? And when had
Billy ever given any suggestion of his Terp-
sichorean abilities — before or since? Were
there any "points" of the kind to be dis-
cerned in him now? None! Was it not
more probable that the Reverend Mr. Withholder had himself been dancing with Polly,
and been mistaken for the goat? Passengers who could have been so deceived with

regard to Polly's beauty might have as easily mistaken the minister for Billy. About this time another incident occurred which increased the mystery.

The only male in the settlement who apparently dissented from the popular opinion regarding Polly was a new-comer, Jack Filgee. While discrediting her performance with the goat, — which he had never seen, — he was evidently greatly prepossessed with the girl herself. Unfortunately, he was equally addicted to drinking, and as he was exceedingly shy and timid when sober, and quite unpresentable at other times, his wooing, if it could be so called, progressed but slowly. Yet when he found that Polly went to church, he listened so far to the exhortations of the Reverend Mr. Withholder as to promise to come to " Bible class " immediately after the Sunday service. It was a hot afternoon, and Jack, who had kept sober for two days, incautiously fortified himself for the ordeal by taking a drink before arriving. He was nervously early, and immediately took a seat in the empty church near the open door. The quiet of the building, the drowsy buzzing of flies, and per-

haps the soporific effect of the liquor caused
his eyes to close and his head to fall forward
on his breast repeatedly. He was recovering himself for the fourth time when he
suddenly received a violent cuff on the ear,
and was knocked backward off the bench
on which he was sitting. That was all he
knew.

He picked himself up with a certain dignity, partly new to him, and partly the result of his condition, and staggered, somewhat bruised and disheveled, to the nearest
saloon. Here a few frequenters who had
seen him pass, who knew his errand and the
devotion to Polly which had induced it, exhibited a natural concern.

" How 's things down at the gospel
shop ? " said one. " Look as ef you 'd been
wrastlin' with the Sperit, Jack ! "

" Old man must hev exhorted pow'ful,"
said another, glancing at his disordered
Sunday attire.

" Ain't be'n hevin' a row with Polly ?
I 'm told she slings an awful left."

Jack, instead of replying, poured out a
dram of whiskey, drank it, and putting down
his glass, leaned heavily against the counter

as he surveyed his questioners with a sorrow chastened by reproachful dignity.

"I'm a stranger here, gentlemen," he said slowly; "ye've known me only a little; but ez ye've seen me both blind drunk and sober, I reckon ye've caught on to my gin'ral gait! Now I wanter put it to you, ez fair-minded men, ef you ever saw me strike a parson?"

"No," said a chorus of sympathetic voices. The barkeeper, however, with a swift recollection of Polly and the Reverend Withholder, and some possible contingent jealousy in Jack, added prudently, "Not yet."

The chorus instantly added reflectively, "Well, no; not yet."

"Did ye ever," continued Jack solemnly, "know me to cuss, sass, bully-rag, or say anything agin parsons, or the church?"

"No," said the crowd, overthrowing prudence in curiosity, "ye never did, — we swear it! And now, what's up?"

"I ain't what you call 'a member in good standin','" he went on, artistically protracting his climax. "I ain't be'n convicted o' sin; I ain't 'a meek an' lowly follower;'

I ain't be'n exactly what I orter be'n; I hev n't lived anywhere up to my lights; but is thet a reason why a parson should strike me?"

"Why? What? When did he? Who did?" asked the eager crowd, with one voice.

Jack then painfully related how he had been invited by the Reverend Mr. Withholder to attend the Bible class. How he had arrived early, and found the church empty. How he had taken a seat near the door to be handy when the parson came. How he just felt "kinder kam and good," listenin' to the flies buzzing, and must have fallen asleep, — only he pulled himself up every time, — though, after all, it war n't no crime to fall asleep in an empty church! How "all of a suddent" the parson came in, "give him a clip side o' the head," and knocked him off the bench, and left him there!

"But what did he *say?*" queried the crowd.

"Nuthin'. Afore I could get up, he got away."

"Are you sure it was him?" they asked. "You know you *say* you was asleep."

"Am I sure?" repeated Jack scornfully. "Don't I know thet face and beard? Did n't I feel it hangin' over me?"

"What are you going to do about it?" continued the crowd eagerly.

"Wait till he comes out — and you'll see," said Jack, with dignity.

This was enough for the crowd; they gathered excitedly at the door, where Jack was already standing, looking towards the church. The moments dragged slowly; it might be a long meeting. Suddenly the church door opened and a figure appeared, looking up and down the street. Jack colored — he recognized Polly — and stepped out into the road. The crowd delicately, but somewhat disappointedly, drew back in the saloon. They did not care to interfere in *that* sort of thing.

Polly saw him, and came hurriedly towards him. She was holding something in her hand.

"I picked this up on the church floor," she said shyly, "so I reckoned you *had* be'n there, — though the parson said you had n't, — and I just excused myself and ran out to give it ye. It's yourn, ain't it?"

She held up a gold specimen pin, which he
had put on in honor of the occasion. " I
had a harder time, though, to git this yer, —
it 's yourn too, — for Billy was laying down
in the yard, back o' the church, and just
comf'bly swallerin' it."

" Who?" said Jack quickly.

" Billy, — my goat."

Jack drew a long breath, and glanced
back at the saloon. " Ye ain't goin' back
to class now, are ye?" he said hurriedly.
" Ef you ain't, I 'll — I 'll see ye home."

" I don't mind," said Polly demurely, " if
it ain't takin' ye outer y'ur way."

Jack offered his arm, and hurrying past
the saloon, the happy pair were soon on the
road to Skinners Pass.

Jack did not, I regret to say, confess his
blunder, but left the Reverend Mr. Withholder to remain under suspicion of having
committed an unprovoked assault and bat-
tery. It was characteristic of Rocky Cañon,
however, that this suspicion, far from injur-
ing his clerical reputation, incited a respect
that had been hitherto denied him. A man
who could hit out straight from the shoulder

had, in the language of the critics, "suthin'
in him." Oddly enough, the crowd that had
at first sympathized with Jack now began to
admit provocations. His subsequent silence,
a disposition when questioned on the subject
to smile inanely, and, later, when insidiously
asked if he had ever seen Polly dancing
with the goat, his bursting into uproarious
laughter completely turned the current of
opinion against him. The public mind, however, soon became engrossed by a more
interesting incident.

The Reverend Mr. Withholder had organ-
ized a series of Biblical tableaux at Skinnerstown for the benefit of his church. Illustra-
tions were to be given of "Rebecca at the
Well," "The Finding of Moses," "Joseph
and his Brethren;" but Rocky Cañon was
more particularly excited by the announcement that Polly Harkness would personate
"Jephthah's Daughter." On the evening
of the performance, however, it was found
that this tableau had been withdrawn and
another substituted, for reasons not given.
Rocky Cañon, naturally indignant at this
omission to represent native talent, indulged
in a hundred wild surmises. But it was

generally believed that Jack Filgee's re-
vengeful animosity to the Reverend Mr.
Withholder was at the bottom of it. Jack,
as usual, smiled inanely, but nothing was to
be got from him. It was not until a few
days later, when another incident crowned
the climax of these mysteries, that a full
disclosure came from his lips.

One morning a flaming poster was displayed at Rocky Cañon, with a charming
picture of the " Sacramento Pet " in the
briefest of skirts, disporting with a tambourine before a goat garlanded with flowers,
who bore, however, an undoubted likeness
to Billy. The text in enormous letters, and
bristling with points of admiration, stated
that the " Pet " would appear as " Esmeralda," assisted by a performing goat, especially trained by the gifted actress. The
goat would dance, play cards, and perform
those tricks of magic familiar to the readers
of Victor Hugo's beautiful story of the
" Hunchback of Notre Dame," and finally
knock down and overthrow the designing
seducer, Captain Phœbus. The marvelous
spectacle would be produced under the pat-
ronage of the Hon. Colonel Starbottle and
the Mayor of Skinnerstown.

As all Rocky Cañon gathered open-
mouthed around the poster, Jack demurely
joined the group. Every eye was turned
upon him.

" It don't look as if yer Polly was in *this*
show, any more than she was in the tablows," said one, trying to conceal his curiosity under a slight sneer. " She don't seem
to be doin' any dancin'!"

" She never *did* any dancin'," said Jack,
with a smile.

" Never *did!* Then what was all these
yarns about her dancin' up at the pass?"

" It was the Sacramento Pet who did all
the dancin'; Polly only *lent* the goat. Ye
see, the Pet kinder took a shine to Billy
arter he bowled Starbottle over thet day at
the hotel, and she thought she might teach
him tricks. So she *did*, doing all her
teachin' and stage-rehearsin' up there at the
pass, so 's to be outer sight, and keep this
thing dark. She bribed Polly to lend her
the goat and keep her secret, and Polly
never let on a word to anybody but me."

" Then it was the Pet that Yuba Bill
saw dancin' from the coach?"

" Yes."

"And that yer artist from New York painted as an 'Imp and Satire'?"

"Yes."

"Then that's how Polly did n't show up in them tablows at Skinnerstown? It was Withholder who kinder smelt a rat, eh? and found out it was only a theayter gal all along that did the dancin'?"

"Well, you see," said Jack, with affected hesitation, "thet's another yarn. I don't know mebbe ez I oughter tell it. Et ain't got anything to do with this advertisement o' the Pet, and might be rough on old man Withholder! Ye must n't ask me, boys."

But there was that in his eye, and above all in this lazy procrastination of the true humorist when he is approaching his climax, which rendered the crowd clamorous and unappeasable. They *would* have the story!

Seeing which, Jack leaned back against a rock with great gravity, put his hands in his pockets, looked discontentedly at the ground, and began: "You see, boys, old Parson Withholder had heard all these yarns about Polly and thet trick-goat, and he kinder reckoned that she might do for some one of his tablows. So he axed her

if she'd mind standin' with the goat and
a tambourine for Jephthah's Daughter, at
about the time when old Jeph comes home,
sailin' in and vowin' he'll kill the first thing
he sees, — jest as it is in the Bible story.
Well, Polly did n't like to say it was n't *her*
that performed with the goat, but the Pet,
for thet would give the Pet dead away; so
Polly agrees to come thar with the goat
and rehearse the tablow. Well, Polly's
thar, a little shy; and Billy, — you bet *he's*
all there, and ready for the fun; but the
darned fool who plays Jephthah ain't worth
shucks, and when *he* comes in he does
nothin' but grin at Polly and seem skeert
at the goat. This makes old Withholder
jest wild, and at last he goes on the platform hisself to show them how the thing
oughter be done. So he comes bustlin' and
prancin' in, and ketches sight o' Polly
dancin' in with the goat to welcome him;
and then he clasps his hands — so — and
drops on his knees, and hangs down his
head — so — and sez, 'Me chyld! me vow!
Oh, heavens!' But jest then Billy —
who's gettin' rather tired o' all this foolishness — kinder slues round on his hind legs,

and ketches sight o' the parson!" Jack paused a moment, and thrusting his hands still deeper in his pockets, said lazily, "I don't know if you fellers have noticed how much old Withholder looks like Billy?"

There was a rapid and impatient chorus of "Yes! yes!" and "Go on!"

"Well," continued Jack, "when Billy sees Withholder kneelin' thar with his head down, he gives a kind o' joyous leap and claps his hoofs together, ez much ez to say, 'I'm on in this scene,' drops his own head, and jest lights out for the parson!"

"And butts him clean through the side scenes into the street," interrupted a delighted auditor.

But Jack's face never changed. "Ye think so?" he said gravely. "But thet's jest whar ye slip up; and thet's jest whar Billy slipped up!" he added slowly. "Mebbe ye've noticed, too, thet the parson's built kinder solid about the head and shoulders. It mought hev be'n thet, or thet Billy did n't get a fair start, but thet goat went down on his fore legs like a shot, and the parson gave one heave, and jest scooted him off the platform! Then the parson reckoned thet this

yer 'tablow' had better be left out, as thar
did n't seem to be any other man who could
play Jephthah, and it was n't dignified for
him to take the part. But the parson
allowed thet it might be a great moral lesson
to Billy!"

And it *was*, for from that moment Billy
never attempted to butt again. He performed with great docility later on in the
Pet's engagement at Skinnerstown; he
played a distinguished rôle throughout the
provinces; he had had the advantages of
Art from "the Pet," and of Simplicity
from Polly, but only Rocky Cañon knew
that his real education had come with his
first rehearsal with the Reverend Mr. Withholder.

DICK SPINDLER'S FAMILY
CHRISTMAS

THERE was surprise and sometimes dis-
appointment in Rough and Ready, when it
was known that Dick Spindler intended to
give a " family " Christmas party at his
own house. That he should take an early
opportunity to celebrate his good fortune
and show hospitality was only expected from
the man who had just made a handsome
" strike " on his claim; but that it should
assume so conservative, old-fashioned, and
respectable a form was quite unlooked-for
by Rough and Ready, and was thought by
some a trifle pretentious. There were not
half-a-dozen families in Rough and Ready;
nobody ever knew before that Spindler had
any relations, and this " ringing in " of
strangers to the settlement seemed to indicate at least a lack of public spirit. " He
might," urged one of his critics, " hev given
the boys, — that had worked alongside o'
him in the ditches by day, and slung lies

with him around the camp-fire by night, — he might hev given them a square ' blow out,' and kep' the leavin's for his old Spindler crew, just as other families do.   Why, when old man Scudder had his house-raisin' last year, his family lived for a week on what was left over, arter the boys had waltzed through the house that night, — and the Scudders warn't strangers, either."   It was also evident that there was an uneasy feeling that Spindler's action indicated an unhallowed leaning towards the minority of respectability and exclusiveness, and a desertion — without the excuse of matrimony — of the convivial and independent bachelor majority of Rough and Ready.

" Ef he was stuck after some gal and was kinder looking ahead, I 'd hev understood it," argued another critic.

" Don't ye be too sure he ain't," said Uncle Jim Starbuck gloomily.   " Ye 'll find that some blamed woman is at the bottom of this yer ' family ' gathering.   That and trouble ez almost all they 're made for ! "

There happened to be some truth in this dark prophecy, but none of the kind that

the misogynist supposed. In fact, Spindler
had called a few evenings before at the
house of the Rev. Mr. Saltover, and Mrs.
Saltover, having one of her " Saleratus
headaches," had turned him over to her
widow sister, Mrs. Huldy Price, who obediently bestowed upon him that practical and
critical attention which she divided with
the stocking she was darning. She was a
woman of thirty-five, of singular nerve and
practical wisdom, who had once smuggled
her wounded husband home from a border
affray, calmly made coffee for his deceived
pursuers while he lay hidden in the loft,
walked four miles for that medical assistance which arrived too late to save him,
buried him secretly in his own "quarter
section," with only one other witness and
mourner, and so saved her position and property in that wild community, who believed
he had fled. There was very little of this
experience to be traced in her round, fresh-
colored brunette cheek, her calm black eyes,
set in a prickly hedge of stiff lashes, her
plump figure, or her frank, courageous
laugh. The latter appeared as a smile
when she welcomed Mr. Spindler. " She

had n't seen him for a coon's age," but " reckoned he was busy fixin' up his new house."

" Well, yes," said Spindler, with a slight hesitation, " ye see, I 'm reckonin' to hev a kinder Christmas gatherin' of my " — he was about to say " folks," but dismissed it for " relations," and finally settled upon " relatives " as being more correct in a preacher's house.

Mrs. Price thought it a very good idea. Christmas was the natural season for the family to gather to " see who 's here and who 's there, who 's gettin' on and who is n't, and who 's dead and buried. It was lucky for them who were so placed that they could do so and be joyful." Her invincible philosophy probably carried her past any dangerous recollections of the lonely grave in Kansas, and holding up the stocking to the light, she glanced cheerfully along its level to Mr. Spindler's embarrassed face by the fire.

" Well, I can't say much ez to that," responded Spindler, still awkwardly, " for you see I don't know much about it anyway."

" How long since you 've seen 'em ? "

asked Mrs. Price, apparently addressing herself to the stocking.

Spindler gave a weak laugh. " Well, you see, ef it comes to that, I 've never seen 'em ! "

Mrs. Price put the stocking in her lap and opened her direct eyes on Spindler. " Never seen 'em ? " she repeated. " Then, they 're not near relations ? "

" There are three cousins," said Spindler, checking them off on his fingers, " a half-uncle, a kind of brother-in-law, — that is, the brother of my sister-in-law's second husband, — and a niece. That 's six."

" But if you 've not seen them, I suppose they 've corresponded with you ? " said Mrs. Price.

" They 've nearly all of 'em written to me for money, seeing my name in the paper ez hevin' made a strike," returned Spindler simply; " and hevin' sent it, I jest know their addresses."

" Oh ! " said Mrs. Price, returning to the stocking.

Something in the tone of her ejaculation increased Spindler's embarrassment, but it also made him desperate. " You see,

Mrs. Price," he blurted out, "I oughter tell ye that I reckon they are the folks that 'hevn't got on,' don't you see, and so it seemed only the square thing for me, ez had 'got on,' to give them a sort o' Christmas festival. Suthin', don't ye know, like what your brother-in-law was sayin' last Sunday in the pulpit about this yer peace and goodwill 'twixt man and man."

Mrs. Price looked again at the man before her. His sallow, perplexed face exhibited some doubt, yet a certain determination, regarding the prospect the quotation had opened to him. "A very good idea, Mr. Spindler, and one that does you great credit," she said gravely.

"I'm mighty glad to hear you say so, Mrs. Price," he said, with an accent of great relief, "for I reckoned to ask you a great favor! You see," he fell into his former hesitation, "that is — the fact is — that this sort o' thing is rather suddent to me, — a little outer my line, don't you see, and I was goin' to ask ye ef you'd mind takin' the hull thing in hand and runnin' it for me."

"Running it for you," said Mrs. Price,

with a quick eye-shot from under the edge
of her lashes. "Man alive! What are you
thinking of?"

"Bossin' the whole job for me," hurried
on Spindler, with nervous desperation.
"Gettin' together all the things and makin'
ready for 'em, — orderin' in everythin' that's
wanted, and fixin' up the rooms, — I kin
step out while you're doin' it, — and then
helpin' me receivin' 'em, and sittin' at the
head o' the table, you know, — like ez ef
you was the mistress."

"But," said Mrs. Price, with her frank
laugh, "that's the duty of one of your relations, — your niece, for instance, — or
cousin, if one of them is a woman."

"But," persisted Spindler, "you see,
they're strangers to me; I don't know 'em,
and I do you. You'd make it easy for 'em,
— and for me, — don't you see? Kinder
introduce 'em, — don't you know? A woman of your gin'ral experience would smooth
down all them little difficulties," continued
Spindler, with a vague recollection of the
Kansas story, "and put everybody on velvet. Don't say 'No,' Mrs. Price! I'm
just kalkilatin' on you."

Sincerity and persistency in a man goes a great way with even the best of women. Mrs. Price, who had at first received Spindler's request as an amusing originality, now began to incline secretly towards it. And, of course, began to suggest objections.

"I'm afraid it won't do," she said thoughtfully, awakening to the fact that it would do and could be done. "You see, I've promised to spend Christmas at Sacramento with my nieces from Baltimore. And then there's Mrs. Saltover and my sister to consult."

But here Spindler's simple face showed such signs of distress that the widow declared she would "think it over," — a process which the sanguine Spindler seemed to consider so nearly akin to talking it over that Mrs. Price began to believe it herself, as he hopefully departed.

She "thought it over" sufficiently to go to Sacramento and excuse herself to her nieces. But here she permitted herself to "talk it over," to the infinite delight of those Baltimore girls, who thought this extravaganza of Spindler's "so Californian and eccentric!" So that it was not strange that presently the news came back to Rough and Ready, and his old associates learned for the first time that he had never seen his relatives, and that they would be doubly strangers. This did not increase his popularity; neither, I grieve to say, did the intelligence that his relatives were probably poor, and that the Reverend Mr. Saltover had approved of his course, and had likened it to the rich man's feast, to which the halt and blind were invited. Indeed, the allusion was supposed to add hypocrisy and a bid for popularity to Spindler's defection, for it was argued that he might have feasted "Wall-eyed Joe" or "Tangle-foot Billy," — who had once been "chawed" by a bear while prospecting, — if he had been sincere. Howbeit, Spindler's faith was oblivious to these criticisms, in his joy at Mr. Saltover's adhesion to his plans and the loan of Mrs. Price as a hostess. In fact, he proposed to her that the invitation should also convey that information in the expression, "by the kind permission of the Rev. Mr. Saltover," as a guarantee of good faith, but the widow would have none of it. The invitations were duly written and dispatched.

"Suppose," suggested Spindler, with a sudden lugubrious apprehension, — "suppose they should n't come?"

"Have no fear, of that," said Mrs. Price, with a frank laugh.

"Or ef they was dead," continued Spindler.

"They could n't all be dead," said the widow cheerfully.

"I 've written to another cousin by marriage," said Spindler dubiously, "in case of accident; I did n't think of him before, because he was rich."

"And have you ever seen him either, Mr. Spindler?" asked the widow, with a slight mischievousness.

"Lordy! No!" he responded, with unaffected concern.

Only one mistake was made by Mrs. Price in her arrangements for the party. She had noticed what the simple-minded Spindler could never have conceived, — the feeling towards him held by his old associates, and had tactfully suggested that a general invitation should be extended to them in the evening.

"You can have refreshments, you know,

too, after the dinner, and games and music."

" But," said the unsophisticated host, " won't the boys think I 'm playing it rather low down on them, so to speak, givin' 'em a kind o' second table, as ef it was the tailings after a strike ? "

" Nonsense," said Mrs. Price, with decision. " It 's quite fashionable in San Francisco, and just the thing to do."

To this decision Spindler, in his blind faith in the widow's management, weakly yielded. An announcement in the " Weekly Banner " that, " On Christmas evening Richard Spindler, Esq., proposed to entertain his friends and fellow citizens at an ' at home,' in his own residence," not only widened the breach between him and the " boys," but awakened an active resentment that only waited for an outlet. It was understood that they were all coming ; but that they should have " some fun out of it " which might not coincide with Spindler's nor his relatives' sense of humor seemed a foregone conclusion.

Unfortunately, too, subsequent events lent themselves to this irony of the situation.

A few mornings after the invitations were dispatched, Spindler, at one of his daily conferences with Mrs. Price, took a newspaper from his pocket. "It seems," he said, looking at her with an embarrassed gravity, "that we will have to take one o' them names off that list, — the name o' Sam Spindler, — and kalkilate upon only six relations coming."

"Ah," said Mrs. Price interestedly, "then you have had an answer, and he has declined?"

"Not that exactly," said Spindler slowly, "but from remarks in this yer paper, he was hung last week by the Vigilance Committee of Yolo."

Mrs. Price opened her eyes on Spindler's face as she took the paper from his hand. "But," she said quickly, "this may be all a mistake, some other Spindler! You know, you say you 've never seen them!"

"I reckon it 's no mistake," said Spindler, with patient gravity, "for the Committee sent me back my invitation, with the kinder disparagin' remark that they 've 'sent him where it ain't bin the habit to keep Christmas!'"

Mrs. Price gasped, but a glance at Spindler's patient, wistful, inquiring eyes brought back her old courage. " Well," she said cheerfully, " perhaps it 's just as well he did n't come."

" Are ye sure o' that, Mrs. Price? " said Spindler, with a slightly troubled expression. " Seems to me, now, that he was the sort as might hev bin gathered in at the feast, and kinder snatched like a brand from the burnin', accordin' to Scripter. But ye know best."

" Mr. Spindler," said Mrs. Price suddenly, with a slight snap in her black eyes, " are your — are the others like this? Or " — here her eyes softened again, and her laugh returned, albeit slightly hysterical — " is this kind of thing likely to happen again? "

" I think we 're pretty sartin o' hevin' six to dinner," returned Spindler simply. Then, as if noticing some other significance in her speech, he added wistfully, " But you won't go back on me, Mrs. Price, ef things ain't pannin' out exackly as I reckoned? You see, I never really knew these yer relations."

He was so obviously sincere in his intent, and, above all, seemed to place such a pathetic reliance on her judgment, that she hesitated to let him know the shock his revelation had given her. And what might his other relations prove to be? Good Lord! Yet, oddly enough, she was so prepossessed by him, and so fascinated by his very Quixotism, that it was perhaps for these complex reasons that she said a little stiffly: —

"One of these cousins, I see, is a lady, and then there is your niece. Do you know anything about them, Mr. Spindler?"

His face grew serious. "No more than I know of the others," he said apologetically. After a moment's hesitation he went on: "Now you speak of it, it seems to me I've heard that my niece was di-vorced. But," he added, brightening up, "I've heard that she was popular."

Mrs. Price gave a short laugh, and was silent for a few minutes. Then this sublime little woman looked up at him. What he might have seen in her eyes was more than he expected, or, I fear, deserved. "Cheer up, Mr. Spindler," she said manfully. "I'll see you through this thing, don't you mind! But don't you say anything about — about — this Vigilance Committee business to anybody. Nor about your niece — it was your niece, was n't it? — being divorced. Charley (the late Mr. Price) had a queer sort of sister, who — but that's neither here nor there! And your niece may n't come, you know; or if she does, you ain't bound to bring her out to the general company."

At parting, Spindler, in sheer gratefulness, pressed her hand, and lingered so long over it that a little color sprang into the widow's brown cheek. Perhaps a fresh courage sprang into her heart, too, for she went to Sacramento the next day, previously enjoining Spindler on no account to show any answers he might receive. At Sacramento her nieces flew to her with confidences.

" We so wanted to see you, Aunt Huldy, for we 've heard something so delightful about your funny Christmas Party! " Mrs. Price's heart sank, but her eyes snapped. " Only think of it! One of Mr. Spindler's long-lost relatives — a Mr. Wragg — lives in this hotel, and papa knows him. He 's a sort of half-uncle, I believe, and he 's just

furious that Spindler should have invited
him. He showed papa the letter; said it
was the greatest piece of insolence in the
world; that Spindler was an ostentatious
fool, who had made a little money and
wanted to use him to get into society; and
the fun of the whole thing was that this
half-uncle and whole brute is himself a par-
venu, — a vulgar, ostentatious creature, who
was only a " —

"Never mind what he was, Kate," interrupted Mrs. Price hastily. "I call his conduct a shame."

"So do we," said both girls eagerly.
After a pause Kate clasped her knees with
her locked fingers, and rocking backwards
and forwards, said, " Milly and I have got
an idea, and don't you say 'No' to it.
We've had it ever since that brute talked
in that way. Now, through him, we know
more about this Mr. Spindler's family con-
nections than you do; and we know all the
trouble you and he'll have in getting up
this party. You understand? Now, we
first want to know what Spindler's like.
Is he a savage, bearded creature, like the
miners we saw on the boat?"

Mrs. Price said that, on the contrary, he was very gentle, soft-spoken, and rather good-looking.

" Young or old ? "

" Young, — in fact, a mere boy, as you may judge from his actions," returned Mrs. Price, with a suggestive matronly air.

Kate here put up a long-handled eyeglass to her fine gray eyes, fitted it ostentatiously over her aquiline nose, and then said, in a voice of simulated horror, " Aunt Huldy, — this revelation is shocking ! "

Mrs. Price laughed her usual frank laugh, albeit her brown cheek took upon it a faint tint of Indian red. " If that 's the wonderful idea you girls have got, I don't see how it 's going to help matters," she said dryly.

" No, that 's not it ! We really have an idea. Now look here."

Mrs. Price " looked here." This process seemed to the superficial observer to be merely submitting her waist and shoulders to the arms of her nieces, and her ears to their confidential and coaxing voices.

Twice she said " it could n't be thought of," and " it was impossible ; " once addressed Kate as " You limb!" and finally said that she "would n't promise, but might write!"

.   .   .   .

It was two days before Christmas. There was nothing in the air, sky, or landscape of that Sierran slope to suggest the season to the Eastern stranger. A soft rain had been dropping for a week on laurel, pine, and buckeye, and the blades of springing grasses and shyly opening flowers. Sedate and silent hillsides that had grown dumb and parched towards the end of the dry season became gently articulate again; there were murmurs in hushed and forgotten cañons, the leap and laugh of water among the dry bones of dusty creeks, and the full song of the larger forks and rivers. Southwest winds brought the warm odor of the pine sap swelling in the forest, or the faint, far-off spice of wild mustard springing in the lower valleys. But, as if by some irony of Nature, this gentle invasion of spring in the wild wood brought only disturbance and discomfort to the haunts and works of man. The ditches were overflowed, the fords of the Fork impassable, the sluicing adrift, and the trails and wagon roads to Rough and Ready knee-deep in mud. The stage-coach from Sacramento, entering the settlement by the mountain highway, its wheels and panels clogged and crusted with an unctuous pigment like mud and blood, passed out of it through the overflowed and dangerous ford, and emerged in spotless purity, leaving its stains behind with Rough and Ready. A week of enforced idleness on the river " Bar " had driven the miners to the more comfortable recreation of the saloon bar, its mirrors, its florid paintings, its armchairs, and its stove. The steam of their wet boots and the smoke of their pipes hung over the latter like the sacrificial incense from an altar. But the attitude of the men was more critical and censorious than contented, and showed little of the gentleness of the weather or season.

" Did you hear if the stage brought down any more relations of Spindler's ? "

The barkeeper, to whom this question was addressed, shifted his lounging position against the bar and said, " I reckon not, ez far ez I know."

" And that old bloat of a second cousin —

that crimson beak — what kem down yesterday, — he ain't bin hangin' round here today for his reg'lar pizon ? "

" No," said the barkeeper thoughtfully, " I reckon Spindler's got him locked up, and is settin' on him to keep him sober till after Christmas, and prevent you boys gettin' at him."

" He'll have the jimjams before that," returned the first speaker ; " and how about that dead beat of a half-nephew who borrowed twenty dollars of Yuba Bill on the way down, and then wanted to get off at Shootersville, but Bill would n't let him, and scooted him down to Spindler's and collected the money from Spindler himself afore he'd give him up ? "

" He's up thar with the rest of the menagerie," said the barkeeper, " but I reckon that Mrs. Price hez bin feedin' him up. And ye know the old woman — that fifty-fifth cousin by marriage — whom Joe Chandler swears he remembers ez an old cook for a Chinese restaurant in Stockton, — darn my skin ef that Mrs. Price has n't rigged her out in some fancy duds of her own, and made her look quite decent."

A deep groan here broke from Uncle Jim Starbuck.

"Did n't I tell ye?" he said, turning appealingly to the others. "It's that darned widow that's at the bottom of it all! She first put Spindler up to givin' the party, and now, darn my skin, ef she ain't goin' to fix up these ragamuffins and drill 'em so we can't get any fun outer 'em after all! And it's bein' a woman that's bossin' the job, and not Spindler, we've got to draw things mighty fine and not cut up too rough, or some of the boys will kick."

"You bet," said a surly but decided voice in the crowd.

"And," said another voice, "Mrs. Price did n't live in 'Bleeding Kansas' for nothing."

"Wot's the programme you've settled on, Uncle Jim?" said the barkeeper lightly, to check what seemed to promise a dangerous discussion.

"Well," said Starbuck, "we kalkilate to gather early Christmas night in Hooper's Hollow and rig ourselves up Injun fashion, and then start for Spindler's with pitchpine torches, and have a 'torchlight dance' around the house; them who does the dancin' and yellin' outside takin' their turn at goin' in and hevin' refreshment. Jake Cooledge, of Boston, sez if anybody objects to it, we've only got to say we're 'Mummers of the Olden Times,' *sabe?* Then, later, we'll have 'Them Sabbath Evening Bells' performed on prospectin' pans by the band. Then, at the finish, Jake Cooledge is goin' to give one of his surkastic specches, — kinder welcomin' Spindler's family to the Free Openin' o' Spindler's Almshouse and Reformatory." He paused, possibly for that approbation which, however, did not seem to come spontaneously. "It ain't much," he added apologetically, "for we're hampered by women; but we'll add to the programme ez we see how things pan out. Ye see, from what we can hear, all of Spindler's relations ain't on hand yet! We've got to wait, like in elekshun times, for 'returus from the back counties.' Hello! What's that?"

It was the swish and splutter of hoofs on the road before the door. The Sacramento coach! In an instant every man was expectant, and Starbuck darted outside on the platform. Then there was the usual greeting and bustle, the hurried ingress of thirsty passengers into the saloon, and a pause. Uncle Jim returned, excitedly and pantingly. " Look yer, boys! Ef this ain't the richest thing out! They say there 's two more relations o' Spindler's on the coach, come down as express freight, consigned, — d' ye hear? — consigned to Spindler! "

" Stiffs, in coffins?" suggested an eager voice.

" I did n't get to hear more. But here they are."

There was the sudden irruption of a laughing, curious crowd into the bar-room, led by Yuba Bill, the driver. Then the crowd parted, and out of their midst stepped two children, a boy and a girl, the oldest apparently of not more than six years, holding each other's hands. They were coarsely yet cleanly dressed, and with a certain uniform precision that suggested formal charity. But more remarkable than all, around the neck of each was a little steel chain, from which depended the regular check and label of the powerful Express Company, Wells, Fargo & Co., and the words: " To Richard Spindler." "Fragile." "With great care." "Collect on delivery." Occasionally their little hands went up automatically and touched their labels, as if to show them. They surveyed the crowd, the floor, the gilded bar, and Yuba Bill without fear and without wonder. There was a pathetic suggestion that they were accustomed to this observation.

"Now, Bobby," said Yuba Bill, leaning back against the bar, with an air half-paternal, half-managerial, "tell these gents how you came here."

"By Wellth, Fargoth Expreth," lisped Bobby.

"Whar from?"

"Wed Hill, Owegon."

"Red Hill, Oregon? Why, it's a thousand miles from here," said a bystander.

"I reckon," said Yuba Bill coolly, "they kem by stage to Portland, by steamer to 'Frisco, steamer again to Stockton, and then by stage over the whole line. Allers by Wells, Fargo & Co.'s Express, from agent to agent, and from messenger to messenger. Fact! They ain't bin tetched or handled by any one but the Kempany's agents; they ain't had a line or direction except them checks around their necks! And they've wanted for nothin' else. Why, I've carried heaps o' treasure before, gentlemen, and once a hundred thousand dollars in greenbacks, but I never carried anythin' that was watched and guarded as them kids! Why, the division inspector at Stockton wanted to go with 'em over the line; but Jim Bracy, the messenger, said he'd call it a reflection on himself and resign, ef they didn't give 'em to him with the other packages! Ye had a pretty good time, Bobby, didn't ye? Plenty to eat and drink, eh?"

The two children laughed a little weak laugh, turned each other bashfully around, and then looked up shyly at Yuba Bill and said, "Yeth."

"Do you know where you are goin'?" asked Starbuck, in a constrained voice.

It was the little girl who answered quickly and eagerly: —

"Yes, to Krissmass and Sandy Claus."

"To what?" asked Starbuck.

Here the boy interposed with a superior air: —

"Thee meanth Couthin Dick. He 'th got Krithmath."

" Where 's your mother? "

" Dead."

" And your father? "

" In orthpittal."

There was a laugh somewhere on the outskirts of the crowd. Every one faced angrily in that direction, but the laugher had disappeared. Yuba Bill, however, sent his voice after him. " Yes, in hospital! Funny, ain't it? — amoosin' place! Try it. Step over here, and in five minutes, by the living Hoky, I 'll qualify you for admission, and not charge you a cent! " He stopped, gave a sweeping glance of dissatisfaction around him, and then, leaning back against the bar, beckoned to some one near the door, and said in a disgusted tone, " You tell these galoots how it happened, Bracy. They make me sick! "

Thus appealed to, Bracy, the express messenger, stepped forward in Yuba Bill's place.

" It 's nothing particular, gentlemen," he said, with a laugh, " only it seems that some man called Spindler, who lives about here, sent an invitation to the father of these children to bring his family to a Christmas

party. It was n't a bad sort of thing for
Spindler to do, considering that they were
his poor relations, though they did n't know
him from Adam, — was it ? " He paused ;
several of the bystanders cleared their
throats, but said nothing. " At least," resumed Bracy, " that 's what the boys up at
Red Hill, Oregon, thought, when they heard
of it. Well, as the father was in hospital
with a broken leg, and the mother only a
few weeks dead, the boys thought it mighty
rough on these poor kids if they were done
out of their fun because they had no one to
bring them. The boys could n't afford to go
themselves, but they got a little money together, and then got the idea of sendin' 'em
by express. Our agent at Red Hill tumbled
to the idea at once ; but he would n't take
any money in advance, and said he would
send 'em ' C. O. D.' like any other package. And he did, and here they are !
That 's all ! And now, gentlemen, as I 've
got to deliver them personally to this Spindler, and get his receipt and take off their
checks, I reckon we must toddle. Come,
Bill, help take 'em up ! "

" Hold on ! " said a dozen voices. A

dozen hands were thrust into a dozen pockets;
I grieve to say some were regretfully withdrawn empty, for it was a hard season in
Rough and Ready. But the expressman
stepped before them, with warning, uplifted
hand.

" Not a cent, boys, — not a cent ! Wells,
Fargo's Express Company don't undertake
to carry bullion with those kids, at least on
the same contract ! " He laughed, and then
looking around him, said confidentially in a
lower voice, which, however, was quite audi-
ble to the children, " There 's as much as
three bags of silver in quarter and half dollars in my treasure box in the coach that
has been poured, yes, just showered upon
them, ever since they started, and have been
passed over from agent to agent and messenger to messenger, — enough to pay their
passage from here to China ! It 's time to
say quits now. But bet your life, they are
not going to that Christmas party poor ! "

He caught up the boy, as Yuba Bill lifted
the little girl to his shoulder, and both
passed out. Then one by one the loungers
in the bar-room silently and awkwardly
followed, and when the barkeeper turned

back from putting away his decanters and
glasses, to his astonishment the room was
empty.

.   .   .   .

Spindler's house, or " Spindler's Splurge,"
as Rough and Ready chose to call it, stood
above the settlement, on a deforested hillside, which, however, revenged itself by
producing not enough vegetation to cover
even the few stumps that were ineradicable.
A large wooden structure in the pseudo-
classic style affected by Westerners, with an
incongruous cupola, it was oddly enough relieved by a still more incongruous veranda
extending around its four sides, upheld by
wooden Doric columns, which were already
picturesquely covered with flowering vines
and sun-loving roses. Mr. Spindler had
trusted the furnishing of its interior to the
same contractor who had upholstered the
gilded bar-room of the Eureka Saloon, and
who had apparently bestowed the same de-
sign and material, impartially, on each.
There were gilded mirrors all over the
house and chilly marble-topped tables, gilt
plaster Cupids in the corners, and stuccoed
lions " in the way " everywhere. The tact-

ful hands of Mrs. Price had screened some of these with seasonable laurels, fir boughs, and berries, and had imparted a slight Christmas flavor to the house. But the greater part of her time had been employed in trying to subdue the eccentricities of Spindler's amazing relations ; in tranquilizing Mrs. "Aunt" Martha Spindler, — the elderly cook before alluded to, — who was inclined to regard the gilded splendors of the house as indicative of dangerous immorality; in restraining "Cousin" Morley Hewlett from considering the dining-room buffet as a bar for "intermittent refreshment ; " and in keeping the weak-minded nephew, Phinney Spindler, from shooting at bottles from the veranda, wearing his uncle's clothes, or running up an account in his uncle's name for various articles at the general stores. Yet the unlooked-for arrival of the two children had been the one great compensation and diversion for her. She wrote at once to her nieces a brief account of her miraculous deliverance. "I think these poor children dropped from the skies here to make our Christmas party possible, to say nothing of the sympathy they have created in Rough

and Ready for Spindler. He is going to
keep them as long as he can, and is writing
to the father. Think of the poor little tots
traveling a thousand miles to ' Krissmass,'
as they call it! — though they were so well
cared for by the messengers that their little
bodies were positively stuffed like quails. So,
you see, dear, we will be able to get along
without airing your famous idea. I 'm sorry,
for I know you 're just dying to see it all."

Whatever Kate's " idea " might have
been, there certainly seemed now no need of
any extraneous aid to Mrs. Price's management. Christmas came at last, and the
dinner passed off without serious disaster.
But the ordeal of the reception of Rough
and Ready was still to come. For Mrs.
Price well knew that although " the boys "
were more subdued, and, indeed, inclined
to sympathize with their host's uncouth
endeavor, there was still much in the aspect
of Spindler's relations to excite their sense
of the ludicrous.

But here Fortune again favored the house
of Spindler with a dramatic surprise, even
greater than the advent of the children had
been. In the change that had come over

Rough and Ready, " the boys " had decided,
out of deference to the women and children,
to omit the first part of their programme,
and had approached and entered the house
as soberly and quietly as ordinary guests.
But before they had shaken hands with the
host and hostess, and seen the relations, the
clatter of wheels was heard before the open
door, and its lights flashed upon a carriage
and pair, — an actual private carriage, —
the like of which had not been seen since
the governor of the State had come down
to open the new ditch! Then there was a
pause, the flash of the carriage lamps upon
white silk, the light tread of a satin foot on
the veranda and in the hall, and the entrance
of a vision of loveliness! Middle-aged
men and old dwellers of cities remembered
their youth ; younger men bethought themselves of Cinderella and the Prince! There
was a thrill and a hush as this last guest —
a beautiful girl, radiant with youth and
adornment — put a dainty glass to her
sparkling eye and advanced familiarly, with
outstretched hand, to Dick Spindler. Mrs.
Price gave a single gasp, and drew back
speechless.

"Uncle Dick," said a laughing contralto voice, which, indeed, somewhat recalled Mrs. Price's own, in its courageous frankness, "I am so delighted to come, even if a little late, and so sorry that Mr. M'Kenna could not come on account of business."

Everybody listened eagerly, but none more eagerly and surprisingly than the host himself. M'Kenna! The rich cousin who had never answered the invitation! And Uncle Dick! This, then, was his divorced niece! Yet even in his astonishment he remembered that of course no one but himself and Mrs. Price knew it, — and that lady had glanced discreetly away.

"Yes," continued the half-niece brightly. "I came from Sacramento with some friends to Shootersville, and from thence I drove here ; and though I must return to-night, I could not forego the pleasure of coming, if it was only for an hour or two, to answer the invitation of the uncle I have not seen for years." She paused, and, raising her glasses, turned a politely questioning eye towards Mrs. Price. "One of our relations?" she said smilingly to Spindler.

"No," said Spindler, with some embarrassment, "a — a friend!"

The half-niece extended her hand. Mrs. Price took it.

But the fair stranger, — what she did and said were the only things remembered in Rough and Ready on that festive occasion; no one thought of the other relations; no one recalled them nor their eccentricities; Spindler himself was forgotten. People only recollected how Spindler's lovely niece lavished her smiles and courtesies on every one, and brought to her feet particularly the misogynist Starbuck and the sarcastic Cooledge, oblivious of his previous speech; how she sat at the piano and sang like an angel, hushing the most hilarious and excited into sentimental and even maudlin silence; how, graceful as a nymph, she led with "Uncle Dick" a Virginia reel until the whole assembly joined, eager for a passing touch of her dainty hand in its changes; how, when two hours had passed, — all too swiftly for the guests, — they stood with bared heads and glistening eyes on the veranda to see the fairy coach whirl the fairy princess away! How — but this incident was never known to Rough and Ready.

It happened in the sacred dressing-room,

where Mrs. Price was cloaking with her own hands the departing half-niece of Mr. Spindler. Taking that opportunity to seize the lovely relative by the shoulders and shake her violently, she said: "Oh, yes, and it's all very well for you, Kate, you limb! For you're going away, and will never see Rough and Ready and poor Spindler again. But what am I to do, miss? How am I to face it out? `For you know I've got to tell him at least that you're no half-niece of his!"

"Have you?" said the young lady.

"Have I?" repeated the widow impatiently. "Have I? Of course I have! What are you thinking of?"

"I was thinking, aunty," said the girl audaciously, "that from what I've seen and heard to-night, if I'm not his half-niece now, it's only a question of time! So you'd better wait. Good-night, dear."

And, really, — it turned out that she was right!

WHEN THE WATERS WERE UP AT "JULES'"

WHEN the waters were up at "Jules'" there was little else up on that monotonous level. For the few inhabitants who calmly and methodically moved to higher ground, camping out in tents until the flood had subsided, left no distracting wreckage behind them. A dozen half-submerged log cabins dotted the tranquil surface of the waters, without ripple or disturbance, looking in the moonlight more like the ruins of centuries than of a few days. There was no current to sap their slight foundations or sweep them away; nothing stirred that silent lake but the occasional shot-like indentations of a passing raindrop, or, still more rarely, a raft, made of a single log, propelled by some citizen on a tour of inspection of his cabin roof-tree, where some of his goods were still stored. There was no sense of terror in this bland obliteration of the little settlement; the ruins of a single burnt-up cabin would have been more impressive than this stupid and even grotesquely placid effect of the rival destroying element. People took it naturally; the water went as it had come, — slowly, impassively, noiselessly; a few days of fervid Californian sunshine dried the cabins, and in a week or two the red dust lay again as thickly before their doors as the winter mud had lain. The waters of Rattlesnake Creek dropped below its banks, the stage-coach from Marysville no longer made a detour of the settlement. There was even a singular compensation to this amicable invasion; the inhabitants sometimes found gold in those breaches in the banks made by the overflow. To wait for the "old Rattlesnake sluicing" was a vernal hope of the trusting miner.

The history of "Jules'," however, was once destined to offer a singular interruption of this peaceful and methodical process. The winter of 1859–60 was an exceptional one. But little rain had fallen in the valleys, although the snow lay deep in the high Sierras. Passes were choked, ravines filled, and glaciers found on their slopes. And when the tardy rains came with the with-

held southwesterly "trades," the regular
phenomenon recurred; Jules' Flat silently,
noiselessly, and peacefully went under water;
the inhabitants moved to the higher ground,
perhaps a little more expeditiously from an
impatience born of the delay. The stage-
coach from Marysville made its usual detour
and stopped before the temporary hotel, express offices, and general store of "Jules',"
under canvas, bark, and the limp leaves of
a spreading alder. It deposited a single
passenger, — Miles Hemmingway, of San
Francisco, but originally of Boston, — the
young secretary of a mining company, dispatched to report upon the alleged auriferous value of "Jules'." Of this he had been
by no means impressed as he looked down
upon the submerged cabins from the box-
seat of the coach and listened to the driver's
lazy recital of the flood, and of the singularly patient acceptance of it by the inhabitants.

It was the old story of the southwestern
miner's indolence and incompetency, — utterly distasteful to his northern habits of
thought and education. Here was their old
fatuous endurance of Nature's wild caprices,

without that struggle against them which brought others strength and success; here was the old philosophy which accepted the prairie fire and cyclone, and survived them without advancement, yet without repining. Perhaps in different places and surroundings a submission so stoic might have impressed him; in gentlemen who tucked their dirty trousers in their muddy boots and lived only for the gold they dug, it did not seem to him heroic. Nor was he mollified as he stood beside the rude refreshment bar — a few planks laid on trestles — and drank his coffee beneath the dripping canvas roof, with an odd recollection of his boyhood and an inclement Sunday-school picnic. Yet these men had been living in this shiftless fashion for three weeks! It exasperated him still more to think that he might have to wait there a few days longer for the water to subside sufficiently for him to make his examination and report. As he took a proffered seat on a candle-box, which tilted under him, and another survey of the feeble makeshifts around him, his irascibility found vent.

"Why, in the name of God, did n't you,

after you had been flooded out *once*, build your cabins *permanently* on higher ground?"

Although the tone of his voice was more disturbing than his question, it pleased one of the loungers to affect to take it literally.

" Well, ez you've put it that way, — ' in the name of God!' " — returned the man lazily, " it mout hev struck us that ez *He* was bossin' the job, so to speak, and handlin' things round here generally, we might leave it to Him.   It was n't *our* flood to monkey with."

" And as He did n't coven-ant, so to speak, to look arter this higher ground 'speshally, and make an Ararat of it for us, ez far ez we could see, we did n't see any reason for *settlin'* yer," put in a second speaker, with equal laziness.

The secretary saw his mistake instantly, and had experience enough of Western humor not to prolong the disadvantage of his unfortunate adjuration.   He colored slightly and said, with a smile, " You know what I mean ; you could have protected yourselves better.   A levee on the bank would have kept you clear of the highest watermark."

"Hev you ever heard *what* the highest

watermark was?" said the first speaker,
turning to another of the loungers without
looking at the secretary.

" Never heard it, — did n't know there was
a limit before," responded the man.

The first speaker turned back to the secretary. " Did you ever know what happened
at ' Bulger's,' on the North Fork? They
had one o' them levees."

" No. What happened? " asked the secretary impatiently.

" They was fixed suthin' like us," returned
the first speaker. " *They* allowed they 'd
build a levee above *their* highest watermark,
and did. It worked like a charm at first;
but the water hed to go somewhere, and it
kinder collected at the first bend. Then it
sorter raised itself on its elbows one day,
and looked over the levee down upon whar
some of the boys was washin' quite comf'ble.
Then it paid no sorter attention to the limit
o' that high watermark, but went six inches
better ! Not slow and quiet like ez it useter
to, ez it does *here*, kinder fillin' up from below, but went over with a rush and a current, hevin' of course the whole height of
the levee to fall on t' other side where

the boys were sluicing." He paused, and amidst a profound silence added, "They say that 'Bulger's' was scattered promiscu-ous-like all along the fort for five miles. I only know that one of his mules and a section of sluicing was picked up at Red Flat, eight miles away!"

Mr. Hemmingway felt that there *was* an answer to this, but, being wise, also felt that it would be unavailing. He smiled politely and said nothing, at which the first speaker turned to him : —

"Thar ain't anything to see to-day, but to-morrow, ez things go, the water oughter be droppin'. Mebbe you'd like to wash up now and clean yourself," he added, with a glance at Hemmingway's small portman-teau. "Ez we thought you'd likely be crowded here, we've rigged up a corner for you at Stanton's shanty with the women."

The young man's cheek flushed slightly at some possible irony in this, and he protested with considerable stress that he was quite ready "to rough it" where he was.

"I reckon it's already fixed," returned the man decisively, "so you'd better come and I'll show you the way."

" One moment," said Hemmingway, with
a smile; " my credentials are addressed to
the manager of the Boone Ditch Company
at ' Jules'.' Perhaps I ought to see him
first."

" All right; he 's Stanton."

" And " — hesitated the secretary, " *you*,
who appear to understand the locality so
well, — I trust I may have the pleasure " —

" Oh, I 'm Jules."

The secretary was a little startled and
amused. So " Jules" was a person, and
not a place !

" Then you 're a pioneer? " asked Hemmingway, a little less dictatorially, as they
passed out under the dripping trees.

" I struck this creek in the fall of '49,
comin' over Livermore's Pass with Stanton,"
returned Jules, with great brevity of speech
and deliberate tardiness of delivery. " Sent
for my wife and two children the next year;
wife died same winter, change bein' too sudden for her, and contractin' chills and fever
at Sweetwater. When I kem here first thar
was n't six inches o' water in the creek;
but there was a heap of it over there where
you see them yallowish-green patches and

strips o' brush and grass; all that war water then, and all that growth hez sprung up since."

Hemmingway looked around him. The "higher ground" where they stood was in reality only a mound-like elevation above the dead level of the flat, and the few trees were merely recent young willows and alders. The area of actual depression was much greater than he had imagined, and its resemblance to the bed of some prehistoric inland sea struck him forcibly. A previous larger inundation than Jules' brief experience had ever known had been by no means improbable. His cheek reddened at his previous hasty indictment of the settlers' ignorance and shiftlessness, and the thought that he had probably committed his employers to his own rash confidence and superiority of judgment. However, there was no evidence that this diluvial record was not of the remote past. He smiled again with greater security as he thought of the geological changes that had since tempered these cataclysms, and the amelioration brought by settlement and cultivation. Nevertheless, he would make a thorough examination tomorrow.

Stanton's cabin was the furthest of these temporary habitations, and was partly on the declivity which began to slope to the river's bank. It was, like the others, a rough shanty of unplaned boards, but, unlike the others, it had a base of logs laid lengthwise on the ground and parallel with each other, on which the flooring and structure were securely fastened. This gave it the appearance of a box slid on runners, or a Noah's Ark whose bulk had been reduced. Jules explained that the logs, laid in that manner, kept the shanty warmer and free from damp. In reply to Hemmingway's suggestion that it was a great waste of material, Jules simply replied that the logs were the " flotsam and jetsam " of the creek from the overflowed mills below.

Hemmingway again smiled. It was again the old story of Western waste and prodigality. Accompanied by Jules, however, he climbed up the huge, slippery logs which made a platform before the door, and entered.

The single room was unequally divided; the larger part containing three beds, by day rolled in a single pile in one corner to make room for a table and chairs. A few dresses hanging from nails on the wall showed that it was the women's room. The smaller compartment was again subdivided by a hanging blanket, behind which was a rude bunk or berth against the wall, a table made of a packing-box, containing a tin basin and a can of water. This was his apartment.

"The women-folks are down the creek, bakin', to-day," said Jules explanatorily; "but I reckon that one of 'em will be up here in a jiffy to make supper, so you just take it easy till they come. I 've got to meander over to the claim afore *I* turn in, but you just lie by to-night and take a rest."

He turned away, leaving Hemmingway standing in the doorway still distraught and hesitating. Nor did the young man recognize the delicacy of Jules' leave-taking until he had unstrapped his portmanteau and found himself alone, free to make his toilet, unembarrassed by company. But even then he would have preferred the rough companionship of the miners in the common dormitory of the general store to this intrusion upon the half-civilization of the women, their pitiable little comforts and secret makeshifts. His disgust of his own indecision which brought him there naturally recoiled in the direction of his host and hostesses, and after a hurried ablution, a change of linen, and an attempt to remove the stains of travel from his clothes, he strode out impatiently into the open air again.

It was singularly mild even for the season. The southwest trades blew softly, and whispered to him of San Francisco and the distant Pacific, with its long, steady swell. He turned again to the overflowed Flat beneath him, and the sluggish yellow water that scarcely broke a ripple against the walls of the half-submerged cabins. And this was the water for whose going down they were waiting with an immobility as tranquil as the waters themselves! What marvelous incompetency, — or what infinite patience! He knew, of course, their expected compensation in this "ground sluicing" at Nature's own hand; the long rifts in the banks of the creek which so often showed "the color" in the sparkling scales of river gold disclosed by the action of the

water; the heaps of reddish mud left after
its subsidence around the walls of the cabins,
— a deposit that often contained a treasure
a dozen times more valuable than the cabin
itself! And then he heard behind him a
laugh, a short and panting breath, and turning, beheld a young woman running towards
him.

In his first astounded sight of her, in her
limp nankeen sunbonnet, thrown back from
her head by the impetus of her flight, he
saw only too much hair, two much white
teeth, too much eye-flash, and, above all, —
as it appeared to him, — too much confidence
in the power of these qualities. Even as
she ran, it seemed to him that she was pull-
ing down ostentatiously the rolled-up sleeves
of her pink calico gown over her shapely
arms. I am inclined to think that the
young gentleman's temper was at fault, and
his conclusion hasty; a calmer observer
would have detected nothing of this in her
frankly cheerful voice. Nevertheless, her
evident pleasure in the meeting seemed to
him only obtrusive coquetry.

"Lordy! I reckoned to git here afore
you 'd get through fixin' up, and in time to

do a little prinkin' myself, and here you're out already." She laughed, glancing at his clean shirt and damp hair. " But all the same, we kin have a talk, and you kin tell me all the news afore the other wimmen get up here. It's a coon's age since I was at Sacramento and saw anybody or anything." She stopped and, instinctively detecting some vague reticence in the man before her, said, still laughing, "You're Mr. Hemmingway, ain't you?"

Hemmingway took off his hat quickly, with a slight start at his forgetfulness. "I beg your pardon; yes, certainly."

"Aunty Stanton thought it was 'Hummingbird,'" said the girl, with a laugh, "but I reckoned not. I'm Jinney Jules, you know; folks call me 'J. J.' It wouldn't do for a Hummingbird and a Jay Jay to be in the same camp, would it? It would be just *too* funny!"

Hemmingway did not find the humor of this so singularly exhaustive, but he was already beginning to be ashamed of his attitude towards her. "I'm very sorry to be giving you all this trouble by my intrusion, for I was quite willing to stay at the store

yonder. Indeed," he added, with a burst
of frankness quite as sincere as her own, " if
you think your father will not be offended,
I would gladly go there now."

If he still believed in her coquetry and
vanity, he would have been undeceived and
crushed by the equal and sincere frankness
with which she met this ungallant speech.

" No! I reckon he would n't care, if
you 'd be as comf'ble and fit for to-morrow.
But ye *would n't,*" she said reflectively.
" The boys thar sit up late over euchre, and
swear a heap, and Simpson, who 'd sleep
alongside of ye, snores pow'ful, I 've heard.
Aunty Stanton kin do her level at that, too,
and they say " —with a laugh — " that *I*
kin, too, but you 're away off in that corner,
and it won't reach you. So, takin' it all,
by the large, you 'd better stay whar ye
are. We wimmen, that is, the most of us,
will be off and away down to Rattlesnake
Bar shoppin' afore sun up, so ye 'll sleep ez
long ez ye want to, and find yer breakfast
ready when ye wake. So I 'll jest set to
and get ye some supper, and ye kin tell me
all the doin's in Sacramento and 'Frisco
while I 'm workin'."

In spite of her unconscious rebuff to his own vanity, Hemmingway felt a sense of relief and less constraint in his relations to this decidedly provincial hostess.

" Can I help you in any way? " he asked eagerly.

" Well, ye *might* bring me an armful o' wood from the pile under the alders, ef ye ain't afraid o' dirtyin' your coat," she said tentatively.

Mr. Hemmingway was not afraid ; he declared himself delighted. He brought a generous armful of small cut willow boughs, and deposited them before a small stove, which seemed a temporary substitute for the usual large adobe chimney that generally occupied the entire gable of a miner's cabin. An elbow and short length of stovepipe carried the smoke through the cabin side. But he also noticed that his fair companion had used the interval to put on a pair of white cuffs and a collar. However, she brushed the green moss from his sleeve with some toweling, and although this operation brought her so near to him that her breath — as soft and warm as the southwest trades — stirred his hair, it was evi-

dent that this contiguity was only frontier
familiarity, as far removed from conscious
coquetry as it was, perhaps, from educated
delicacy.

"The boys gin'rally kem to take up
enough wood for me to begin with," she
said, " but I reckon they did n't know I was
comin' up so soon."

Hemmingway's distrust returned a little
at this obvious suggestion that he was only
a substitute for their general gallantry, but
he smiled and said somewhat bluntly, " I
don't suppose you lack for admirers here."

The girl, however, took him literally.
"Lordy, no! Me and Mamie Robinson
are the only girls for fifteen miles along
the creek. *Admirin' !* I call it jest *pes-
terin'* sometimes! I reckon I 'll hev to keep
a dog!"

Hemmingway shivered. Yes, she was
not only conscious, but spoilt already. He
pictured to himself the uncouth gallantries
of the settlement, the provincial badinage,
the feeble rivalries of the young men whom
he had seen at the general store. Undoubtedly this was what she was expecting in
him!

"Well," she said, turning from the fire she had kindled, "while I'm settin' the table, tell me what's a-doin' in Sacramento! I reckon you've got heaps of lady friends thar, — I'm told there's lots of fashions just from the States."

"I'm afraid I don't know enough of them to interest you," he said dryly.

"Go on and talk," she replied. "Why, when Tom Flynn kem back from Sacramento, and he war n't thar more nor a week, he jest slung yarns about his doin's thar to last the hull rainy season."

Half amused and half annoyed, Hemmingway seated himself on the little platform beside the open door, and began a conscientious description of the progress of Sacramento, its new buildings, hotels, and theatres, as it had struck him on his last visit. For a while he was somewhat entertained by the girl's vivacity and eager questioning, but presently it began to pall. He continued, however, with a grim sense of duty, and partly as a reason for watching her in her household duties. Certainly she was graceful! Her tall, lithe, but beautifully moulded figure, even in its characteristic southwestern indolence, fell into poses as picturesque as they were unconscious. She lifted the big molasses-can from its shelf on the rafters with the attitude of a Greek water-bearer. She upheaved the heavy flour-sack to the same secure shelf with the upraised palms of an Egyptian caryatid. Suddenly she interrupted Hemmingway's perfunctory talk with a hearty laugh. He started, looked up from his seat on the platform, and saw that she was standing over him and regarding him with a kind of mischievous pity.

"Look here," she said, "I reckon that'll do! You kin pull up short! I kin see what's the matter with you; you're jest plumb tired, tuckered out, and want to turn in! So jest you sit that quiet until I get supper ready and never mind me." In vain Hemmingway protested, with a rising color. The girl only shook her head. "Don't tell me! You ain't keering to talk, and you're only playin' Sacramento statistics on me," she retorted, with unfeigned cheerfulness. "Anyhow, here's the wimmen comin', and supper is ready."

There was a sound of weary, resigned

ejaculations and pantings, and three gaunt
women in lustreless alpaca gowns appeared
before the cabin. They seemed prematurely
aged and worn with labor, anxiety, and ill
nourishment. Doubtless somewhere in these
ruins a flower like Jay Jules had once flour-
ished ; doubtless somewhere in that graceful
nymph herself the germ of this dreary ma-
turity was hidden. Hemmingway welcomed
them with a seriousness equal to their own.
The supper was partaken with the kind of
joyless formality which in the southwest is
supposed to indicate deep respect, even the
cheerful Jay falling under the influence, and
it was with a feeling of relief that at last the
young man retired to his fenced-off corner
for solitude and repose. He gathered, however, that before " sun up " the next morning the elder women were going to Rattlesnake Bar for the weekly shopping, leaving
Jay as before to prepare his breakfast and
then join them later. It was already a
change in his sentiments to find himself
looking forward to that *tête-à-tête* with the
young girl, as a chance of redeeming his
character in her eyes. He was beginning
to feel he had been stupid, unready, and

withal prejudiced. He undressed himself in his seclusion, broken only by the monotonous voices in the adjoining apartment. From time to time he heard fragments and scraps of their conversation, always in reference to affairs of the household and settlement, but never of himself, — not even the suggestion of a prudent lowering of their voices, — and fell asleep. He woke up twice in the night with a sensation of cold so marked and distinct from his experience of the early evening, that he was fain to pile his clothes over his blankets to keep warm. He fell asleep again, coming once more to consciousness with a sense of a slight jar, but relapsing again into slumber for he knew not how long. Then he was fully awakened by a voice calling him, and, opening his eyes, beheld the blanket partition put aside, and the face of Jay thrust forward. To his surprise it wore a look of excited astonishment dominated by irrepressible laughter.

"Get up quick as you kin," she said gaspingly; "this is about the killingest thing that ever happened!"

She disappeared, but he could still hear her laughing, and to his utter astonishment with her disappearance the floor seemed to change its level. A giddy feeling seized him; he put his feet to the floor: it was unmistakably wet and oozing. He hurriedly clothed himself, still accompanied by the strange feeling of oscillation and giddiness, and passed through the opening into the next room. Again his step produced the same effect upon the floor, and he actually stumbled against her shaking figure, as she wiped the tears of uncontrollable mirth from her eyes with her apron. The contact seemed to upset her remaining gravity. She dropped into a chair, and, pointing to the open door, gasped, "Look thar! Lordy! How's that for high?" threw her apron over her head, and gave way to an uproarious fit of laughter.

Hemmingway turned to the open door. A lake was before him on the level of the cabin. He stepped forward on the platform; the water was right and left, all around him. The platform dipped slightly to his step. The cabin was afloat, — afloat upon its base of logs like a raft, the whole structure upheld by the floor on which the logs were securely fastened. The high ground had disappeared

— the river — its banks — the green area beyond. They, and *they* alone, were afloat upon an inland sea.

He turned an astounded and serious face upon her mirth. " When did it happen ? " he demanded. She checked her laugh, more from a sense of polite deference to his mood than any fear, and said quietly, " That gets me.   Everything was all right two hours ago when the wimmen left; It was too early to get your breakfast and rouse ye out, and I fell asleep, I reckon, until I felt a kind o' slump and a jar." Hemmingway remembered his own half-conscious sensation. " Then I got up and saw we was adrift.   I did n't waken ye, for I thought it was only a sort of wave that would pass.   It was n't until I saw we were movin' and the hull rising ground gettin' away, that I thought o' callin' ye."

He thought of the vanished general store, of her father, the workers on the bank, the helpless women on their way to the Bar, and turned almost savagely on her.

" But the others, — where are they ? " he said indignantly. " Do you call that a laughing matter ? "

She stopped at the sound of his voice as at a blow. Her face hardened into immobility, yet when she replied it was with the deliberate indolence of her father. " The wimmen are up on the hills by this time. The boys hev bin drowned out many times afore this and got clear off, on sluice boxes and timber, without squealing. Tom Flynn went down ten miles to Sayer's once on two bar'ls, and I never heard that *he* was cryin' when they picked him up."

A flush came to Hemmingway's cheek, but with it a gleam of intelligence. Of course the inundation was known to them *first*, and there was the wreckage to support them. They had clearly saved themselves. If they had abandoned the cabin, it was because they knew its security, perhaps had even seen it safely adrift.

" Has this ever happened to the cabin before ? " he asked, as he thought of its peculiar base.

" No."

He looked at the water again. There was a decided current. The overflow was evidently no part of the original ·inundation. He put his hand in the water. It was icy

cold. Yes, he understood it now. It was
the sudden melting of snow in the Sierras
which had brought this volume down the
cañon. But was there more still to come?

" Have you anything like a long pole or
stick in the cabin? "

" Nary," said the girl, opening her big
eyes and shaking her head with a simulation of despair, which was, however, flatly
contradicted by her laughing mouth.

" Nor any cord or twine?" he continued.

She handed him a ball of coarse twine.

" May I take a couple of these hooks? "
he asked, pointing to some rough iron hooks
in the rafters, on which bacon and jerked
beef were hanging.

She nodded. He dislodged the hooks,
greased them with the bacon rind, and
affixed them to the twine.

" Fishin'? " she asked demurely.

" Exactly," he replied gravely.

He threw the line in the water. It
slackened at about six feet, straightened,
and became taut at an angle, and then
dragged. After one or two sharp jerks he
pulled it up. A few leaves and grasses
were caught in the hooks. He examined
them attentively.

"We're not in the creek," he said, "nor in the old overflow. There's no mud or gravel on the hooks, and these grasses don't grow near water."

"Now, that's mighty cute of you," she said admiringly, as she knelt beside him on the platform. "Let's see what you've caught. Look yer!" she added, suddenly lifting a limp stalk, "that's 'old man,' and thar ain't a scrap of it grows nearer than Springer's Rise, — four miles from home."

"Are you sure?" he asked quickly.

"Sure as pop! I used to go huntin' it for smellidge."

"For what?" he said, with a bewildered smile.

"For this," — she thrust the leaves to his nose and then to her own pink nostrils; "for — for" — she hesitated, and then with a mischievous simulation of correctness added, "for the perfume."

He looked at her admiringly. For all her five feet ten inches, what a mere child she was, after all! What a fool he was to have taken a resentful attitude towards her! How charming and graceful she looked, kneeling there beside him!

" Tell me," he said suddenly, in a gentler voice, "what were you laughing at just now?"

Her brown eyes wavered for a moment, and then brimmed with merriment. She threw herself sideways, in a leaning posture, supporting herself on one arm, while with her other hand she slowly drew out her apron string, as she said, in a demure voice: —

" Well, I reckoned it was jest too killin' to think of you, who did n't want to talk to me, and would hev given your hull pile to hev skipped out o' this, jest stuck here alongside o' me, whether you would or no, for Lord knows how long!"

" But that was last night," he said, in a tone of raillery. "I was tired, and you said so yourself, you know. But I'm ready to talk now. What shall I tell you?"

" Anything," said the girl, with a laugh.

" What I am thinking of?" he said, with frankly admiring eyes.

" Yes."

" Everything?"

" Yes, everything." She stopped, and leaning forward, suddenly caught the brim of his soft felt hat, and drawing it down smartly over his audacious eyes, said, "Everything *but that*."

It was with some difficulty and some greater embarrassment that he succeeded in getting his eyes free again. When he did so, she had risen and entered the cabin. Disconcerted as he was, he was relieved to see that her expression of amusement was unchanged. Was her act a piece of rustic coquetry, or had she resented his advances? Nor did her next words settle the question.

"Ye kin do yer nice talk and philanderin' after we've settled whar we are, whar we're goin', and what's goin' to happen. Jest now it 'pears to me that ez these yere logs are the only thing betwixt us and 'kingdom come,' ye'd better be hustlin' round with a few spikes to clinch 'em to the floor."

She handed him a hammer and a few spikes. He obediently set to work, with little confidence, however, in the security of the fastening. There was neither rope nor chain for lashing the logs together; a stronger current and a collision with some submerged stump or wreckage would loosen them and wreck the cabin. But he said nothing. It was the girl who broke the silence.

" What 's your front name ? "

" Miles."

" *Miles*, — that 's a funny name. I reckon that 's why you war so *far off* and *distant* at first."

Mr. Hemmingway thought this very witty, and said so. " But," he added, " when I was a little nearer a moment ago, you stopped me."

" But you was moving faster than the shanty was. I reckon you don't take that gait with your lady friends at Sacramento ! However, you kin talk now."

" But you forget I don't know ' where we are,' nor ' what 's going to happen.' "

" But *I* do," she said quietly. " In a couple of hours we 'll be picked up, so you 'll be free again."

Something in the confidence of her manner made him go to the door again and look out. There was scarcely any current now, and the cabin seemed motionless. Even the wind, which might have acted upon it, was wanting. They were apparently in the same position as before, but his sounding-line showed that the water was slightly falling. He came back and imparted the fact with a certain confidence born of her previous praise of his knowledge. To his surprise she only laughed and said lazily, " We'll be all right, and you'll be free, in about two hours."

" I see no sign of it," he said, looking through the door again.

" That's because you're looking in the water and the sky and the mud for it," she said, with a laugh. " I reckon you've been trained to watch them things a heap better than to study the folks about here."

" I daresay you're right," said Hemming-way cheerfully, " but I don't clearly see what the folks about here have to do with our situation just now."

" You'll see," she said, with a smile of mischievous mystery. " All the same," she added, with a sudden and dangerous softness in her eyes, " I ain't sayin' that *you* ain't kinder right neither."

An hour ago he would have laughed at the thought that a mere look and sentence like this from the girl could have made his heart beat. " Then I may go on and talk ? "

She smiled, but her eyes said, " Yes," plainly.

He turned to take a chair near her. Suddenly the cabin trembled, there was a sound of scraping, a bump, and then the whole structure tilted to one side and they were both thrown violently towards the corner, with a swift inrush of water. Hemmingway quickly caught the girl by the waist; she clung to him instinctively, yet still laughing, as with a desperate effort he succeeded in dragging her to the upper side of the slanting cabin, and momentarily restoring its equilibrium. They remained for an instant breathless. But in that instant he had drawn her face to his and kissed her.

She disengaged herself gently with neither excitement nor emotion, and pointing to the open door said, " Look there ! "

Two of the logs which formed the foundation of their floor were quietly floating in the water before the cabin ! The submerged obstacle or snag which had torn them from

their fastening was still holding the cabin
fast. Hemmingway saw the danger. He
ran along the narrow ledge to the point of
contact and unhesitatingly leaped into the
icy cold water. It reached his armpits before his feet struck the obstacle,— evidently
a stump with a projecting branch. Bracing
himself against it, he shoved off the cabin.
But when he struck out to follow it, he found
that the log nearest him was loose and his
grasp might tear it away. At the same
moment, however, a pink calico arm fluttered
above his head, and a strong grasp seized his
coat collar. The cabin half revolved as the
girl dragged him into the open door.

"You bantam!" she said, with a laugh,
"why did n't you let *me* do that? I 'm
taller than you! But," she added, looking
at his dripping clothes and dragging out a
blanket from the corner, "I could n't dry
myself as quick as you kin!" To her surprise, however, Hemmingway tossed the
blanket aside, and pointing to the floor,
which was already filmed with water, ran to
the still warm stove, detached it from its
pipe, and threw it overboard. The sack of
flour, bacon, molasses, and sugar, and all

the heavier articles followed it into the stream. Relieved of their weight the cabin base rose an inch or two higher. Then he sat down and said, "There! that may keep us afloat for that 'couple of hours' you speak of. So I suppose I may talk now!"

"Ye have n't no time," she said, in a graver voice. "It won't be as long as a couple of hours now. Look over thar!"

He looked where she pointed across the gray expanse of water. At first he could see nothing. Presently he saw a mere dot on its face which at times changed to a single black line.

"It 's a log, like these," he said.

"It 's no log. It 's an Injun dug-out [1]—comin' for me."

"Your father?" he said joyfully.

She smiled pityingly. "It 's Tom Flynn. Father 's got suthin' else to look arter. Tom Flynn has n't."

"And who 's Tom Flynn?" he asked, with an odd sensation.

"The man I 'm engaged to," she said gravely, with a slight color.

---

[1] A canoe made from a hollowed log.

The rose that blossomed on her cheek
faded in his. There was a moment of
silence. Then he said frankly, "I owe you
some apology. Forgive my folly and impertinence a moment ago. How could I
have known this?"

"You took no more than you deserved, or
that Tom would have objected to," she said,
with a little laugh. "You've been mighty
kind and handy."

She held out her hand; their fingers
closed together in a frank pressure. Then
his mind went back to his work, which he
had forgotten, — to his first impressions of
the camp and of her. They both stood
silent, watching the canoe, now quite visible,
and the man that was paddling it, with an
intensity that both felt was insincere.

"I'm afraid," he said, with a forced
laugh, "that I was a little too hasty in dis-
posing of your goods and possessions. We
could have kept afloat a little longer."

"It's all the same," she said, with a
slight laugh; "it's jest as well we did n't
look too comf'ble — to *him*."

He did not reply; he did not dare to look
at her. Yes! It was the same coquette he

had seen last night. His first impressions were correct.

The canoe came on rapidly now, propelled by a powerful arm. In a few moments it was alongside, and its owner leaped on the platform. It was the gentleman with his trousers tucked in his boots, the second voice in the gloomy discussion in the general store last evening. He nodded simply to the girl, and shook Hemmingway's hand warmly.

Then he made a hurried apology for his delay: it was so difficult to find " the lay " of the drifted cabin. He had struck out first for the most dangerous spot, — the " old clearing," on the right bank, with its stumps and new growths, — and it seemed he was right. And all the rest were safe, and " nobody was hurt."

" All the same, Tom," she said, when they were seated and paddling off again, " you don't know *how near you came to losing me*." Then she raised her beautiful eyes and looked significantly, not at *him*, but at Hemmingway.

When the water was down at " Jules' " the next day, they found certain curious changes and some gold, and the secretary was able to make a favorable report. But he made none whatever of his impressions "when the water was up at 'Jules','" though he often wondered if they were strictly trustworthy.

THE BOOM IN THE "CALAVERAS CLARION"

THE editorial sanctum of the "Calaveras Clarion" opened upon the "composing-room" of that paper on the one side, and gave apparently upon the rest of Calaveras County upon the, other. For, situated on the very outskirts of the settlement and the summit of a very steep hill, the pines sloped away from the editorial windows to the long valley of the South Fork and — infinity. The little wooden building had invaded Nature without subduing it. It was filled night and day with the murmur of pines and their fragrance. Squirrels scampered over its roof when it was not preoccupied by woodpeckers, and a printer's devil had once seen a nest-building blue jay enter the composing window, flutter before one of the slanting type-cases with an air of deliberate selection, and then fly off with a vowel in its bill.

Amidst these sylvan surroundings the

temporary editor of the " Clarion " sat at his
sanctum, reading the proofs of an editorial.
As he was occupying that position during a
six weeks' absence of the *bonâ fide* editor
and proprietor, he was consequently reading
the proof with some anxiety and responsibility. It had been suggested to him by certain
citizens that the " Clarion " needed a firmer
and more aggressive policy towards the
Bill before the Legislature for the wagon
road to the South Fork. Several Assembly men had been " got at " by the rival
settlement of Liberty Hill, and a scathing
exposure and denunciation of such methods
was necessary. The interests of their own
township were also to be " whooped up."
All this had been vigorously explained to
him, and he had grasped the spirit, if not
always the facts, of his informants. It is
to be feared, therefore, that he was perus-
ing his article more with reference to its
vigor than his own convictions. And yet
he was not so greatly absorbed as to be
unmindful of the murmur of the pines
without, his half-savage environment, and
the lazy talk of his sole companions, — the
foreman and printer in the adjoining room.

" Bet your life ! I 've always said that a man *inside* a newspaper office could hold his own agin any outsider that wanted to play rough or tried to raid the office ! Thar 's the press, and thar 's the printin' ink and roller ! Folks talk a heap o' the power o' the Press ! — I tell ye, ye don't half know it. Why, when old Kernel Fish was editin' the ' Sierra Banner,' one o' them bullies that he 'd lampooned in the ' Banner' fought his way past the Kernel in the office, into the composin'-room, to wreck everythin' and 'pye' all the types. Spoffrel — ye don't remember Spoffrel ? — little red-haired man ? — was foreman. Spoffrel fended him off with the roller and got one good dab inter his eyes that blinded him, and then Spoffrel sorter skirmished him over to the press, — a plain lever just like ours, — whar the locked-up form of the inside was still a-lyin' ! Then, quick as lightnin', Spoffrel tilts him over agin it, and *he* throws out his hand and ketches hold o' the form to steady himself, when Spoffrel just runs the form and the hand under the press and down with the lever ! And that held the feller fast as grim death ! And when at last he begs off, and Spoff lets him loose, the hull o' that 'ere lampooning article he objected to was printed right onto the skin o' his hand! Fact, and it would n't come off, either."

"Gosh, but I'd like to hev seen it," said the printer. "There ain't any chance, I reckon, o' such a sight here. The boss don't take no risks lampoonin', and he" (the editor knew he was being indicated by some unseen gesture of the unseen workman) "ain't that style."

"Ye never kin tell," said the foreman didactically, "what might happen! . I 've known editors to get into a fight jest for a little innercent bedevilin' o' the opposite party. Sometimes for a misprint. Old man Pritchard of the 'Argus' oncet had a hole blown through his arm because his proof-reader had called Colonel Starbottle's speech an 'ignominious' defense, when the old man hed written 'ingenuous' defense."

The editor paused in his proof-reading. He had just come upon the sentence: "We cannot congratulate Liberty Hill — in its superior elevation — upon the ignominious silence of the representative of all Calaveras when this infamous Bill was introduced."

He referred to his copy. Yes! He had certainly written "ignominious," — that was what his informants had suggested. But was he sure they were right? He had a vague recollection, also, that the representative alluded to — Senator Bradley — had fought two duels, and was a "good" though somewhat impulsive shot! He might alter the word to "ingenuous" or "ingenious," either would be finely sarcastic, but then — there was his foreman, who would detect it! He would wait until he had finished the entire article. In that occupation he became oblivious of the next room, of a silence, a whispered conversation, which ended with a rapping at the door and the appearance of the foreman in the doorway.

"There's a man in the office who wants to see the editor," he said.

"Show him in," replied the editor briefly. He was, however, conscious that there was a singular significance in his foreman's manner, and an eager apparition of the other printer over the foreman's shoulder.

"He's carryin' a shot-gun, and is a man twice as big as you be," said the foreman gravely.

The editor quickly recalled his own brief and as yet blameless record in the " Clarion." " Perhaps," he said tentatively, with a gentle smile, " he 's looking for Captain Brush " (the absent editor).

" I told him all that," said the foreman grimly, " and he said he wanted to see the man in charge."

In proportion as the editor's heart sank his outward crest arose. " Show him in," he said loftily.

" We *kin* keep him out," suggested the foreman, lingering a moment; " me and him," indicating the expectant printer behind him, " is enough for that."

" Show him up," repeated the editor firmly.

The foreman withdrew; the editor seated himself and again took up his proof. The doubtful word " ignominious " seemed to stand out of the paragraph before him; it certainly *was* a strong expression ! He was about to run his pencil through it when he heard the heavy step of his visitor approaching. A sudden instinct of belligerency took possession of him, and he wrathfully threw the pencil down.

The burly form of the stranger blocked the doorway.   He was dressed like a miner, but his build and general physiognomy were quite distinct from the local variety.   His upper lip and chin were clean-shaven, still showing the blue-black roots of the beard which covered the rest of his face and depended in a thick fleece under his throat. He carried a small bundle tied up in a silk handkerchief in one hand, and a " shot-gun " in the other, perilously at half-cock.   Entering the sanctum, he put down his bundle and quietly closed the door behind him. He then drew an empty chair towards him and dropped heavily into it with his gun on his knees.   The editor's heart dropped almost as heavily, although he quite composedly held out his hand.

" Shall I relieve you of your gun ? "

" Thank ye, lad — noa.   It 's moor coomfortable wi' me, and it 's main dangersome to handle on the half-cock.   That 's why I did n't leave 'im on the horse outside ! "

At the sound of his voice and occasional accent a flash of intelligence relieved the editor's mind.   He remembered that twenty miles away, in the illimitable vista from his windows, lay a settlement of English north-country miners, who, while faithfully adopting the methods, customs, and even slang of the Californians, retained many of their native peculiarities. The gun he carried on his knee, however, was evidently part of the Californian imitation.

"Can I do anything for you?" said the editor blandly.

"Ay! I 've coom here to bill ma woife."

"I — don't think I understand," hesitated the editor, with a smile.

"I 've coom here to get ye to put into your paaper a warnin', a notiss, that onless she returns to my house in four weeks, I 'll have nowt to do wi' her again."

"Oh!" said the editor, now perfectly reassured, "you want an advertisement? That 's the business of the foreman; I 'll call him." He was rising from his seat when the stranger laid a heavy hand on his shoulder and gently forced him down again.

"Noa, lad! I don't want noa foreman nor understrappers to take this job. I want to talk it over wi' you. *Sabe?* My woife she bin up and awaa these six months. We had a bit of difference, that ain't here nor there, but she skedaddled outer my house. I want to give her fair warning, and let her know I ain't payin' any debts o' hers arter this notiss, and I ain't takin' her back arter four weeks from date."

" I see," said the editor glibly. " What 's your wife's name ? "

" Eliza Jane Dimmidge."

" Good," continued the editor, scribbling on the paper before him ; " something like this will do : ' Whereas my wife, Eliza Jane Dimmidge, having left my bed and board without just cause or provocation, this is to give notice that I shall not be responsible for any debts of her contracting on or after this date.' "

" Ye must be a lawyer," said Mr. Dimmidge admiringly.

It was an old enough form of advertisement, and the remark showed incontestably that Mr. Dimmidge was not a native ; but the editor smiled patronizingly and went on : " ' And I further give notice that if she does not return within the period of four weeks from this date, I shall take such proceedings for relief as the law affords.' "

" Coom, lad, I did n't say *that*."

"But you said you would n't take her back."

"Ay."

"And you can't prevent her without legal proceedings. She 's your wife. But you need n't take proceedings, you know. It 's only a warning."

Mr. Dimmidge nodded approvingly. "That 's so."

"You 'll want it published for four weeks, until date?" asked the editor.

"Mebbe longer, lad."

The editor wrote "till forbid" in the margin of the paper and smiled.

"How big will it be?" said Mr. Dimmidge.

The editor took up a copy of the "Clarion" and indicated about an inch of space. Mr. Dimmidge's face fell.

"I want it bigger, — in large letters, like a play-card," he said. "That 's no good for a warning."

"You can have half a column or a whole column if you like," said the editor airily.

"I 'll take a whole one," said Mr. Dimmidge simply.

The editor laughed. "Why! it would cost you a hundred dollars."

"I 'll take it," repeated Mr. Dimmidge.

"But," said the editor gravely, "the same notice in a small space will serve your purpose and be quite legal."

"Never you mind that, lad! It 's the looks of the thing I 'm arter, and not the expense. I 'll take that column."

The editor called in the foreman and showed him the copy. "Can you display that so as to fill a column?"

The foreman grasped the situation promptly. It would be big business for the paper. "Yes," he said meditatively, "that bold-faced election type will do it."

Mr. Dimmidge's face brightened. The expression "bold - faced" pleased him. "That 's it! I told you. I want to bill her in a portion of the paper."

"I might put in a cut," said the foreman suggestively; "something like this." He took a venerable woodcut from the case. I grieve to say it was one which, until the middle of the present century, was common enough in the newspaper offices in the Southwest. It showed the running figure of a negro woman carrying her personal property in a knotted handkerchief slung from a stick over her shoulder, and was supposed to represent " a fugitive slave."

Mr. Dimmidge's eyes brightened. " I 'll take that, too. It 's a little dark-complected for Mrs. D., but it will do. Now roon away, lad," he said to the foreman, as he quietly pushed him into the outer office again and closed the door. Then, facing the surprised editor, he said, " Theer 's another notiss I want ye to put in your paper; but that 's atween *us*. Not a word to *them*," he indicated the banished foreman with a jerk of his thumb. " *Sabe?* I want you to put this in another part o' your paper, quite innocent-like, ye know." He drew from his pocket a gray wallet, and taking out a slip of paper read from it gravely, " ' If this should meet the eye of R. B., look out for M. J. D. He is on your track. When this you see write a line to E. J. D., Elktown Post Office.' I want this to go in as ' Personal and Private ' — *sabe?* — like them notisses in the big 'Frisco papers."

" I see," said the editor, laying it aside. " It shall go in the same issue in another column."

Apparently Mr. Dimmidge expected some-

thing more than this reply, for after a moment's hesitation he said with an odd smile :

" Ye ain't seein' the meanin' o' that, lad ? "

" No," said the editor lightly ; " but I suppose R. B. does, and it is n't intended that
any one else should."

" Mebbe it is, and mebbe it is n't," said
Mr. Dimmidge, with a self-satisfied air. " I
don't mind saying atween us that R. B. is
the man as I 've suspicioned as havin' something to do with my wife goin' away ; and ye
see, if he writes to E. J. D. — that 's my
wife's initials — at Elktown, *I 'll* get that
letter and so make sure."

" But suppose your wife goes there first,
or sends ? "

" Then I 'll ketch her or her messenger.
Ye see ? "

The editor did not see fit to oppose any
argument to this phenomenal simplicity, and
Mr. Dimmidge, after settling his bill with
the foreman, and enjoining the editor to the
strictest secrecy regarding the origin of the
" personal notice," took up his gun and departed, leaving the treasury of the " Clarion "
unprecedentedly enriched, and the editor to
his proofs.

The paper duly appeared the next morning with the column advertisement, the personal notice, and the weighty editorial on the wagon road. There was a singular demand for the paper, the edition was speedily exhausted, and the editor was proportionately flattered, although he was surprised to receive neither praise nor criticism from his subscribers. Before evening, however, he learned to his astonishment that the excitement was caused by the column advertisement. Nobody knew Mr. Dimmidge, nor his domestic infelicities, and the editor and foreman, being equally in the dark, took refuge in a mysterious and impressive evasion of all inquiry. Never since the last San Francisco Vigilance Committee had the office been so besieged. The editor, foreman, and even the apprentice, were buttonholed and " treated " at the bar, but to no effect. All that could be learned was that it was a *bonâ fide* advertisement, for which one hundred dollars had been received! There were great discussions and conflicting theories as to whether the value of the wife, or the husband's anxiety to get rid of her, justified the enormous expense and ostenta-

tious display. She was supposed to be an
exceedingly beautiful woman by some, by
others a perfect Sycorax ; in one breath Mr.
Dimmidge was a weak, uxorious spouse,
wasting his substance on a creature who did
not care for him, and in another a maddened,
distracted, henpecked man, content to pur-
chase peace and rest at any price. Certainly,
never was advertisement more effective in its
publicity, or cheaper in proportion to the
circulation it commanded. It was copied
throughout the whole Pacific slope ; mighty
San Francisco papers described its size and
setting under the attractive headline, " How
they Advertise a Wife in the Mountains ! "
It reappeared in the Eastern journals, under
the title of " Whimsicalities of the Western
Press." It was believed to have crossed to
England as a specimen of " Transatlantic
Savagery." The real editor of the " Clarion "
awoke one morning, in San Francisco, to
find his paper famous. Its advertising columns were eagerly sought for ; he at once
advanced the rates. People bought succes-
sive issues to gaze upon this monumental
record of extravagance. A singular idea,
which, however, brought further fortune to

the paper, was advanced by an astute critic
at the Eureka Saloon. " My opinion, gentlemen, is that the whole blamed thing is
a bluff! There ain't no Mr. Dimmidge;
there ain't no Mrs. Dimmidge; there ain't
no desertion! The whole rotten thing is an
advertisement o' suthin'! Ye 'll find afore
ye get through with it that that there wife
won't come back until that blamed husband
buys Somebody's Soap, or treats her to
Somebody's particular Starch or Patent
Medicine! Ye jest watch and see!" The
idea was startling, and seized upon the mer-
cantile mind. The principal merchant of
the town, and purveyor to the mining settlements beyond, appeared the next morning at
the office of the " Clarion." " Ye would n't
mind puttin' this ' ad ' in a column alongside o' the Dimmidge one, would ye ? " The
young editor glanced at it, and then, with a
serpent-like sagacity, veiled, however, by the
suavity of the dove, pointed out that the
original advertiser might think it called his
bonâ fides into question and withdraw his
advertisement. " But if we secured you by
an offer of double the amount per column ? "
urged the merchant. " That," responded the

locum tenens, " was for the actual editor and
proprietor in San Francisco to determine.
He would telegraph." He did so. The re-
sponse was, " Put it in." Whereupon in the
next issue, side by side with Mr. Dimmidge's
protracted warning, appeared a column with
the announcement, in large letters, " *WE*
HAVE N'T LOST ANY WIFE, but WE are
prepared to furnish the following goods at a
lower rate than any other advertiser in the
county," followed by the usual price list of
the merchant's wares. There was an unpre-
cedented demand for that issue. The reputation of the " Clarion," both as a shrewd
advertising medium and a comic paper,
was established at once. For a few days
the editor waited with some apprehension for
a remonstrance from the absent Dimmidge,
but none came. Whether Mr. Dimmidge
recognized that this new advertisement gave
extra publicity to his own, or that he was
already on the track of the fugitive, the editor did not know. The few curious citizens
who had, early in the excitement, penetrated
the settlement of the English miners twenty
miles away in search of information, found
that Mr. Dimmidge had gone away, and that

Mrs. Dimmidge had *never* resided there with him!

Six weeks passed. The limit of Mr. Dimmidge's advertisement had been reached, and, as it was not renewed, it had passed out of the pages of the " Clarion," and with it the merchant's advertisement in the next column. The excitement had subsided, although its influence was still felt in the circulation of the paper and its advertising popularity. The temporary editor was also nearing the limit of his incumbency, but had so far participated in the good fortune of the " Clarion " as to receive an offer from one of the San Francisco dailies.

It was a warm night, and he was alone in his sanctum. The rest of the building was dark and deserted, and his solitary light, flashing out through the open window, fell upon the nearer pines and was lost in the dark, indefinable slope below. He had reached the sanctum by the rear, and a door which he also left open to enjoy the freshness of the aromatic air. Nor did it in the least mar his privacy. Rather the solitude of the great woods without seemed to enter through that door and encompassed him with its protecting loneliness. There was occasionally a faint " peep " in the scant eaves, or a " pat-pat," ending in a frightened scurry across the roof, or the slow flap of a heavy wing in the darkness below. These gentle disturbances did not, however, interrupt his work on " The True Functions of the County Newspaper," the editorial on which he was engaged.

Presently a more distinct rustling against the straggling blackberry bushes beside the door attracted his attention. It was followed by a light tapping against the side of the house. The editor started and turned quickly towards the open door. Two outside steps led to the ground. Standing upon the lower one was a woman. The upper part of her figure, illuminated by the light from the door, was thrown into greater relief by the dark background of the pines. Her face was unknown to him, but it was a pleasant one, marked by a certain good-humored determination.

" May I come in ? " she said confidently.

" Certainly," said the editor. " I am working here alone because it is so quiet." He thought he would precipitate some explanation from her by excusing himself.

" That's the reason why I came," she said, with a quiet smile.

She came up the next step and entered the room. She was plainly but neatly dressed, and now that her figure was revealed he saw that she was wearing a linsey-woolsey riding-skirt, and carried a serviceable rawhide whip in her cotton-gauntleted hand. She took the chair he offered her and sat down sideways on it, her whip hand now also holding up her skirt, and permitting a hem of clean white petticoat and a smart, well-shaped boot to be seen.

" I don't remember to have had the pleasure of seeing you in Calaveras before," said the editor tentatively.

" No. I never was here before," she said composedly, " but you've heard enough of me, I reckon. I'm Mrs. Dimmidge." She threw one hand over the back of the chair, and with the other tapped her riding-whip on the floor.

The editor started. Mrs. Dimmidge! Then she was not a myth. An absurd similarity between her attitude with the whip and her husband's entrance with his gun six weeks before forced itself upon him and made her an invincible presence.

"Then you have returned to your husband?" he said hesitatingly.

"Not much!" she returned, with a slight curl of her lip.

"But you read his advertisement?"

"I saw that column of fool nonsense he put in your paper — ef that's what you mean," she said with decision, "but I didn't come here to see *him* — but *you*."

The editor looked at her with a forced smile, but a vague misgiving. He was alone at night in a deserted part of the settlement, with a plump, self-possessed woman who had a contralto voice, a horsewhip, and — he could not help feeling — an evident grievance.

"To see me?" he repeated, with a faint attempt at gallantry. "You are paying me a great compliment, but really" —

"When I tell you I've come three thousand miles from Kansas straight here without stopping, ye kin reckon it's so," she replied firmly.

"Three thousand miles!" echoed the editor wonderingly.

"Yes. Three thousand miles from my own folks' home in Kansas, where six years ago I married Mr. Dimmidge, — a British furriner as could scarcely make himself understood in any Christian language! Well, he got round me and dad, allowin' he was a reg'lar out-and-out profeshnal miner, — had lived in mines ever since he was a boy; and so, not knowin' what kind o' mines, and dad just bilin' over with the gold fever, we were married and kem across the plains to Californy. He was a good enough man to look at, but it warn't three months before I discovered that he allowed a wife was no better nor a nigger slave, and he the master. That made me open my eyes; but then, as he did n't drink, and did n't gamble, and did n't swear, and was a good provider and laid by money, why I shifted along with him as best I could. We drifted down the first year to Sonora, at Red Dog, where there was n't another woman. Well, I did the nigger slave business, — never stirring out o' the settlement, never seein' a town or a crowd o' decent people, — and he did the lord and master! We played that game for two years, and I got tired. But when at last he allowed he 'd go up to Elktown Hill, where there was a passel o' his countrymen at work, with never a sign o' any other folks, and leave me alone at Red Dog until he fixed up a place for me at Elktown Hill, — I kicked! I gave him fair warning! I did as other nigger slaves did, — I ran away!"

A recollection of the wretched woodcut which Mr. Dimmidge had selected to personify his wife flashed upon the editor with a new meaning. Yet perhaps she had not seen it, and had only read a copy of the advertisement. What could she want? The "Calaveras Clarion," although a "Palladium" and a "Sentinel upon the Heights of Freedom" in reference to wagon roads, was not a redresser of domestic wrongs, — except through its advertising columns! Her next words intensified that suggestion.

" I 've come here to put an advertisement in your paper."

The editor heaved a sigh of relief, as once before. "Certainly," he said briskly. "But that 's another department of the paper, and the printers have gone home. Come to-morrow morning early."

" To-morrow morning I shall be miles away," she said decisively, " and what I want done has got to be done *now!* I don't want to see no printers; I don't want *any-body* to know I've been here but you. That's why I kem here at night, and rode all the way from Sawyer's Station, and would n't take the stage-coach. And when we 've settled about the advertisement, I 'm going to mount my horse, out thar in the bushes, and scoot outer the settlement."

" Very good," said the editor resignedly. " Of course I can deliver your instructions to the foreman. And now — let me see — I suppose you wish to intimate in a personal notice to your husband that you 've returned."

" Nothin' o' the kind! " said Mrs. Dimmidge coolly. " I want to placard him as he did me. I 've got it all written out here. *Sabe ?* "

She took from her pocket a folded paper, and spreading it out on the editor's desk, with a certain pride of authorship read as follows : —

" Whereas my husband, Micah J. Dimmidge, having given out that I have left his bed and board, — the same being a bunk in a log cabin and pork and molasses three times a day, — and having advertised that he 'd pay no debts of *my* contractin', — which, as thar ain't any, might be easier collected than debts of his own contractin', — this is to certify that unless he returns from Elktown Hill to his only home in Sonora in one week from date, payin' the cost of this advertisement, I 'll know the reason why. — Eliza Jane Dimmidge."

"Thar," she added, drawing a long breath, "put that in a column of the 'Clarion,' same size as the last, and let it work, and that 's all I want of you."

"A column?" repeated the editor. "Do you know the cost is very expensive, and I *could* put it in a single paragraph?"

"I reckon I kin pay the same as Mr. Dimmidge did for *his*," said the lady complacently. "I did n't see your paper myself, but the paper as copied it — one of them big New York dailies — said that it took up a whole column."

The editor breathed more freely; she had not seen the infamous woodcut which her husband had selected. At the same moment he was struck with a sense of retribution, justice, and compensation.

"Would you," he asked hesitatingly, — "would you like it illustrated — by a cut?"

" With which ? "

" Wait a moment ; I 'll show you."

He went into the dark composing-room, lit a candle, and rummaging in a drawer sacred to weather-beaten, old-fashioned electrotyped advertising symbols of various trades, finally selected one and brought it to Mrs. Dimmidge. It represented a bare and exceedingly stalwart arm wielding a large hammer.

" Your husband being a miner, — a quartz miner, — would that do ? " he asked. (It had been previously used to advertise a blacksmith, a gold-beater, and a stone-mason.)

The lady examined it critically.

" It does look a little like Micah's arm," she said meditatively. " Well — you kin put it in."

The editor was so well pleased with his success that he must needs make another suggestion. " I suppose," he said ingenuously, " that you don't want to answer the ' Personal ' ? "

" ' Personal ' ? " she repeated quickly, " what 's that ? I ain't seen no ' Personal.' "

The editor saw his blunder. She, of course,

had never seen Mr. Dimmidge's artful " Personal; " *that* the big dailies naturally had not noticed nor copied. But it was too late to withdraw now. He brought out a file of the " Clarion," and snipping out the paragraph with his scissors, laid it before the lady.

She stared at it with wrinkled brows and a darkening face.

" And *this* was in the same paper ? — put in by Mr. Dimmidge ? " she asked breathlessly.

The editor, somewhat alarmed, stammered " Yes." But the next moment he was reassured. The wrinkles disappeared, a dozen dimples broke out where they had been, and the determined, matter-of-fact Mrs. Dimmidge burst into a fit of rosy merriment. Again and again she laughed, shaking the building, startling the sedate, melancholy woods beyond, until the editor himself laughed in sheer vacant sympathy.

" Lordy ! " she said at last, gasping, and wiping the laughter from her wet eyes. " I never thought of *that*."

" No," explained the editor smilingly ; " of course you did n't. Don't you see, the papers that copied the big advertisement never saw that little paragraph, or if they did, they never connected the two together. "

" Oh, it ain't that," said Mrs. Dimmidge, trying to regain her composure and holding her sides. " It 's that blessed *dear* old dunderhead of a Dimmidge I 'm thinking of. That gets me. I see it all now. Only, sakes alive! I never thought *that* of him. Oh, it 's just too much! " and she again relapsed behind her handkerchief.

" Then I suppose you don't want to reply to it," said the editor.

Her laughter instantly ceased. " Don't I ? " she said, wiping her face into its previous complacent determination. " Well, young man, I reckon that 's just what I *want* to do! Now, wait a moment; let 's see what he said," she went on, taking up and reperusing the " Personal " paragraph. " Well, then," she went on, after a moment's silent composition with moving lips, " you just put these lines in."

The editor took up his pencil.

" To Mr. J. D. Dimmidge. — Hope you 're still on R. B.'s tracks. Keep there! — E. J. D."

The editor wrote down the line, and then, remembering Mr. Dimmidge's voluntary explanation of *his* "Personal," waited with some confidence for a like frankness from Mrs. Dimmidge. But he was mistaken.

"You think that he — R. B. — or Mr. Dimmidge — will understand this?" he at last asked tentatively. "Is it enough?"

"Quite enough," said Mrs. Dimmidge emphatically. She took a roll of greenbacks from her pocket, selected a hundred-dollar bill and then a five, and laid them before the editor. "Young man," she said, with a certain demure gravity, "you 've done me a heap o' good. I never spent money with more satisfaction than this. I never thought much o' the ' power o' the Press,' as you call it, afore. But this has been a right comfortable visit, and I 'm glad I ketched you alone. But you understand one thing : this yer visit, and *who* I am, is betwixt you and me only."

"Of course I must say that the advertisement was *authorized*," returned the editor. "I 'm only the temporary editor. The proprietor is away."

" So much the better," said the lady complacently. " You just say you found it on
your desk with the money; but don't you
give me away."

" I can promise you that the secret of
your personal visit is safe with me," said the
young man, with a bow, as Mrs. Dimmidge
rose. " Let me see you to your horse," he
added. " It's quite dark in the woods."

" I can see well enough alone, and it's
just as well you should n't know *how* I
kem or *how* I went away. Enough for you
to know that I'll be miles away before that
paper comes out. So stay where you are."

She pressed his hand frankly and firmly,
gathered up her riding-skirt, slipped backwards to the door, and the next moment
rustled away into the darkness.

Early the next morning the editor handed
Mrs. Dimmidge's advertisement, and the
woodcut he had selected, to his foreman.
He was purposely brief in his directions,
so as to avoid inquiry, and retired to his
sanctum. In the space of a few moments
the foreman entered with a slight embarrassment of manner.

" You 'll excuse my speaking to you, sir,"

he said, with a singular mixture of humility
and cunning. "It's no business of mine,
I know; but I thought I ought to tell you
that this yer kind o' thing won't pay any
more, — it's about played out!"

"I don't think I understand you," said
the editor loftily, but with an inward misgiving. "You don't mean to say that a
regular, actual advertisement"—

"Of course, I know all that," said the
foreman, with a peculiar smile; "and I'm
ready to back you up in it, and so's the boy;
but it won't pay."

"It *has* paid a hundred and five dollars,"
said the editor, taking the notes from his
pocket; "so I'd advise you to simply attend to your duty and set it up."

A look of surprise, followed, however, by
a kind of pitying smile, passed over the
foreman's face. "Of course, sir, *that's* all
right, and you know your own business; but
if you think that the new advertisement will
pay this time as the other one did, and
whoop up another column from an advertiser, I'm afraid you'll slip up. It's a
little 'off color' now, — not 'up to date,' —
if it ain't a regular 'back number,' as
you'll see."

" Meantime I 'll dispense with your advice," said the editor curtly, "and I think
you had better let our subscribers and ad-
vertisers do the same, or the ' Clarion '
might also be obliged to dispense with your
services."

" I ain't no blab," said the foreman, in an
aggrieved manner, "and I don't intend to
give the show away even if it don't *pay*.
But I thought I 'd tell you, because I know
the folks round here better than you do."

He was right. No sooner had the advertisement appeared than the editor found that
everybody believed it to be a sheer inven-
tion of his own to "once more boom " the
" Clarion." If they had doubted *Mr*. Dimmidge, they utterly rejected *Mrs*. Dimmidge
as an advertiser! It was a stale joke that
nobody would follow up; and on the heels
of this came a letter from the editor-in-chief.

MY DEAR BOY, — You meant well, I
know, but the second Dimmidge " ad " was
a mistake. Still, it was a big bluff of yours
to show the money, and I send you back
your hundred dollars, hoping you won't
" do it again." Of course you 'll have to

keep the advertisement in the paper for two issues, just as if it were a real thing, and it's lucky that there's just now no pressure in our columns. You might have told a better story than that hogwash about your finding the " ad " and a hundred dollars lying loose on your desk one morning. It was rather thin, and I don't wonder the fore-man kicked.

The young editor was in despair. At first he thought of writing to Mrs. Dim-midge at the Elktown Post-Office, asking her to relieve him of his vow of secrecy; but his pride forbade. There was a humor-ous concern, not without a touch of pity, in the faces of his contributors as he passed; a few affected to believe in the new adver-tisement, and asked him vague, perfunctory questions about it. His position was trying, and he was not sorry when the term of his engagement expired the next week, and he left Calaveras to take his new position on the San Francisco paper.

He was standing in the saloon of the Sacramento boat when he felt a sudden heavy pressure on his shoulder, and looking round sharply, beheld not only the black-bearded face of Mr. Dimmidge, lit up by a smile, but beside it the beaming, buxom face of Mrs. Dimmidge, overflowing with good-humor. Still a little sore from his past experience, he was about to address them abruptly, when he was utterly vanquished by the hearty pressure of their hands and the unmistakable look of gratitude in their eyes.

" I was just saying to 'Lizy Jane," began Mr. Dimmidge breathlessly, " if I could only meet that young man o' the ' Clarion ' what brought us together again " —

" You 'd be willin' to pay four times the amount we both paid him," interpolated the laughing Mrs. Dimmidge.

" But I did n't bring you together," burst out the dazed young man, " and I 'd like to know, in the name of Heaven, what brought you together now ? "

" Don't you see, lad," said the imperturbable Mr. Dimmidge, " 'Lizy Jane and myself had qua'lled, and we just unpacked our fool nonsense in your paper and let the hull world know it ! And we both felt kinder skeert and shamed like, and it looked such small hogwash, and of so little account, for all the talk it made, that we kinder felt lonely as two separated fools that really ought to share their foolishness together."

" And that ain't all," said Mrs. Dimmidge, with a sly glance at her spouse, " for I found out from that 'Personal' you showed me that this particular old fool was actooally jealous ! —*jealous !* "

" And then ? " said the editor impatiently.

" And then I *knew* he loved me all the time."

THE SECRET OF SOBRIENTE'S WELL

Even to the eye of the most inexperienced traveler there was no doubt that Buena Vista was a "played-out" mining camp. There, seamed and scarred by hydraulic engines, was the old hillside, over whose denuded surface the grass had begun to spring again in fitful patches ; there were the abandoned heaps of tailings already blackened by sun. and rain, and worn into mounds like ruins. of masonry; there were the waterless ditches, like giant graves, and the pools of slumgullion, now dried into shining, glazed cement. There were two or three wooden "stores," from which the windows and doors had been. taken and conveyed to the newer settlement: of Wynyard's Gulch. Four or five buildings that still were inhabited — the blacksmith's shop, the post-office, a pioneer's cabin, and the old hotel and stage-office — only accented the general desolation. The latter building had a remoteness of prosper-

ity far beyond the others, having been a wayside Spanish-American · *posada*, with adobe
walls of two feet in thickness, that shamed
the later shells of half-inch plank, which
were slowly warping and cracking like dried
pods in the oven-like heat.

The proprietor of this building, Colonel
Swinger, had been looked upon by the com·
munity as a person quite as remote, old-
fashioned, and inconsistent with present
progress as the house itself.   He was an old
Virginian, who had emigrated from his decaying plantation on the James River only
to find the slaves, which he had brought
with him, freed men when they touched
Californian soil ; to be driven by Northern
progress and " smartness " out of the larger
cities into the mountains, to fix himself at
last, with the hopeless fatuity of his race,
upon an already impoverished settlement ;
to sink his scant capital in hopeless shafts
and ledges, and finally to take over the
decaying hostelry of Buena Vista, with its
desultory custom and few, lingering, impe-
cunious guests.   Here, too, his old Virginian
ideas of hospitality were against his financial
success ; he could not dun nor turn from his

door those unfortunate prospectors whom the ebbing fortunes of Buena Vista had left stranded by his side.

Colonel Swinger was sitting in a wicker-work rocking-chair on the veranda of his hotel — sipping a mint julep which he held in his hand, while he gazed into the dusty distance. Nothing could have convinced him that he was not performing a serious part of his duty as hotel-keeper in this attitude, even though there were no travelers expected, and the road at this hour of the day was deserted. On a bench at his side Larry Hawkins stretched his lazy length, — one foot dropped on the veranda, and one arm occasionally groping under the bench for his own tumbler of refreshment. Apart from this community of occupation, there was apparently no interchange of sentiment between the pair. The silence had continued for some moments, when the colonel put down his glass and gazed earnestly into the distance.

" Seein' anything? " remarked the man on the bench, who had sleepily regarded him.

" No," said the colonel, " that is — it 's only Dick Ruggles crossin' the road."

" Thought you looked a little startled, ez if you 'd seen that ar wanderin' stranger."

" When I see that wandering stranger, sah," said the colonel decisively, " I won't be sittin' long in this yer chyar. I 'll let him know in about ten seconds that I don't harbor any vagrants prowlin' about like poor whites or free niggers on my propahty, sah ! "

⁓   " All the same, I kinder wish ye did see him, for you 'd be settled in *your* mind and I 'd be easier in *mine*, ef you found out what he was doin' round yer, or ye had to admit that it was n't no *livin'* man."

" What do you mean ? " said the colonel, testily facing around in his chair.

His companion also altered his attitude by dropping his other foot to the floor, sitting up, and leaning lazily forward with his hands clasped.

" Look yer, colonel. When you took this place, I felt I did n't have no call to tell ye all I know about it, nor to pizen yer mind by any darned fool yarns I mout hev heard. Ye know it was one o' them old Spanish *haciendas ?* "

" I know," said the colonel loftily, " that

it was held by a grant from Charles the
Fifth of Spain, just as my propahty on the
James River was given to my people by
King James of England, sah ! "

" That ez as may be," returned his companion, in lazy indifference ; " though I
reckon that Charles the Fifth of Spain and
King James of England ain't got much to
do with what I 'm goin' to tell ye. Ye see,
I was here long afore *your* time, or any of
the boys that hev now cleared out; and at
that time the *hacienda* belonged to a man
named Juan Sobriente. He was that kind
o' fool that he took no stock in mining.
When the boys were whoopin' up the place
and finding the color everywhere, and there
was a hundred men working down there in
the gulch, he was either ridin' round lookin'
up the wild horses he owned, or sittin' with
two or three lazy peons and Injins that was
fed and looked arter by the priests. Gosh !
now I think of it, it was mighty like *you*
when you first kem here with your niggers.
That 's curious, too, ain't it ? "

He had stopped, gazing with an odd,
superstitious wonderment at the colonel, as
if overcome by this not very remarkable

coincidence. The colonel, overlooking or totally oblivious to its somewhat uncomplimentary significance, simply said, " Go on. What about him ? "

" Well, ez I was sayin', he warn't in it nohow, but kept on his reg'lar way when the boom was the biggest. Some of the boys allowed it was mighty oncivil for him to stand off like that, and others — when he refused a big pile for his *hacienda* and the garden, that ran right into the gold-bearing ledge — war for lynching him and driving him outer the settlement. But as he had a pretty darter or niece livin' with him, and, except for his partickler cussedness towards mining, was kinder peaceable and perlite, they thought better of it. Things went along like this, until one day the boys noticed — particklerly the boys that had slipped up on their luck — that old man Sobriente was gettin' rich, — had stocked a ranch over on the Divide, and had given some gold candlesticks to the mission church. That would have been only human nature and business, ef he 'd had any during them flush times ; but he had n't. This kinder puzzled them. They tackled the peons, —

his niggers, — but it was all 'No sabe.'
They tackled another man, — a kind of half-
breed Kanaka, who, except the priest, was
the only man who came to see him, and was
supposed to be mighty sweet on the darter
or niece, — but they did n't even get the
color outer *him*. Then the first thing we
knowed was that old Sobriente was found
dead in the well!"

"In the well, sah!" said the colonel,
starting up. "The well on my propahty?"

"No," said his companion. "The old
well that was afterwards shut up. Yours
was dug by the last tenant, Jack Raintree,
who allowed that he did n't want to 'take any
Sobriente in his reg'lar whiskey and water.'
Well, the half-breed Kanaka cleared out
after the old man's death, and so did that
darter or niece; and the church, to whom
old Sobriente had left this house, let it to
Raintree for next to nothin'."

"I don't see what all that has got to do
with that wandering tramp," said the colonel,
who was by no means pleased with this history of his property.

"I 'll tell ye. A few days after Raintree
took it over, he was lookin' round the gar-

den, which old Sobriente had always kept shut up agin strangers, and he finds a lot of dried-up 'slumgullion' [1] scattered all about the borders and beds, just as if the old man had been using it for fertilizing. Well, Raintree ain't no fool; he allowed the old man was n't one, either; and he knew that slumgullion was n't worth no more than mud for any good it would do the garden. So he put this yer together with Sobriente's good luck, and allowed to himself that the old coyote had been secretly gold-washin' all the while he seemed to be standin' off agin it! But where was the mine? Whar did he get the gold? That 's what got Raintree. He hunted all over the garden, prospected every part of it, — ye kin see the holes yet, — but he never even got the color!"

He paused, and then, as the colonel made an impatient gesture, he went on.

"Well, one night just afore you took the place, and when Raintree was gettin' just sick of it, he happened to be walkin' in the garden. He was puzzlin' his brain agin to know how old Sobriente made his pile, when

---

[1] That is, a viscid cement-like refuse of gold-washing.

all of a suddenst he saw suthin' a-movin' in
the brush beside the house. He calls out,
thinkin' it was one of the boys, but got no
answer. Then he goes to the bushes, and a
tall figger, all in black, starts out afore him.
He could n't see any face, for its head was
covered with a hood, but he saw that it
held suthin' like a big cross clasped agin its
breast. This made him think it was one o'
them priests, until he looks agin and sees
that it was n't no cross it was carryin,' but
a *pickaxe!* He makes a jump towards it,
but it vanished! He traipsed over the hull
garden, — went through ev'ry bush, — but it
was clean gone. Then the hull thing flashed
upon him with a cold shiver. The old man
bein' found dead in the well! the goin'
away of the half-breed and the girl! the
findin' o' that slumgullion! The old man
had made a strike in that garden, the half-
breed had discovered his secret and murdered him, throwin' him down the well!
It war no *livin'* man that he had seen, but
the ghost of old Sobriente!"

The colonel emptied the remaining contents of his glass at a single gulp, and sat
up. "It's my opinion, sah, that Raintree

had that night more than his usual allowance of corn-juice on board; and it's only a wonder, sah, that he did n't see a few pink alligators and sky-blue snakes at the same time. But what's this got to do with that wanderin' tramp?"

"They're all the same thing, colonel, and in my opinion that there tramp ain't no more alive than that figger was."

"But *you* were the one that saw this tramp with your own eyes," retorted the colonel quickly, "and you never before allowed it was a spirit!"

"Exactly! I saw it whar a minit afore nothin' had been standin', and a minit after nothin' stood," said Larry Hawkins, with a certain serious emphasis; "but I warn't goin' to say it to *anybody*, and I warn't goin' to give you and the *hacienda* away. And ez nobody knew Raintree's story, I jest shut up my head. But you kin bet your life that the man I saw warn't no livin' man!"

"We'll see, sah!" said the colonel, rising from his chair with his fingers in the armholes of his nankeen waistcoat, "ef he ever intrudes on my property again. But look yar! don't ye go sayin' anything of this to Polly, — you know what women are!"

A faint color came into Larry's face; an animation quite different to the lazy deliberation of his previous monologue shone in his eyes, as he said, with a certain rough respect he had not shown before to his companion, "That 's why I 'm tellin' ye, so that ef *she* happened to see anything and got skeert, ye 'd know how to reason her out of it."

" 'Sh!" said the colonel, with a warning gesture.

A young girl had just appeared in the doorway, and now stood leaning against the central pillar that supported it, with one hand above her head, in a lazy attitude strongly suggestive of the colonel's Southern indolence, yet with a grace entirely her own. Indeed, it overcame the negligence of her creased and faded yellow cotton frock and unbuttoned collar, and suggested — at least to the eyes of *one* man — the curving and clinging of the jasmine vine against the outer column of the veranda. Larry Hawkins rose awkwardly to his feet.

"Now what are you two men mumblin'

and confidin' to each other? You look for all the world like two old women gossips," she said, with languid impertinence.

It was easy to see that a privileged and recognized autocrat spoke. No one had ever questioned Polly Swinger's right to interrupting, interfering, and saucy criticisms. Secure in the hopeless or chivalrous admiration of the men around her, she had repaid it with a frankness that scorned any coquetry; with an indifference to the ordinary feminine effect or provocation in dress or bearing that was as natural as it was invincible. No one had ever known Polly to " fix up " for anybody, yet no one ever doubted the effect, if she had. No one had ever rebuked her charming petulance, or wished to.

Larry gave a weak, vague laugh. Colonel Swinger as ineffectively assumed a mock parental severity. " When you see two gentlemen, miss, discussin' politics together, it ain't behavin' like a lady to interrupt. Better run away and tidy yourself before the stage comes."

The young lady replied to the last innuendo by taking two spirals of soft hair, like

" corn silk," from her oval cheek, wetting
them with her lips, and tucking them behind
her ears.   Her father's ungentlemanly suggestion being thus disposed of, she returned
to her first charge.

" It ain't no politics ; you ain't been swear-
ing enough for *that !*   Come, now !   It 's
the mysterious stranger ye 've been talking
about ! "

Both men stared at her with unaffected
concern.

" What do *you* know about any mysterious stranger ? " demanded her father.

" Do you suppose you men kin keep a secret," scoffed Polly.   " Why, Dick Ruggles
told me how skeert ye all were over an entire
stranger, and he advised me not to wander
down the road after dark.   I asked him if he
thought I was a pickaninny to be frightened
by bogies, and that if he had n't a better
excuse for wantin' ' to see me home ' from
the Injin spring, he might slide."

Larry laughed again, albeit a little bitterly,
for it seemed to him that the excuse was fully
justified ; but the colonel said promptly,
" Dick 's a fool, and you might have told him
there were worse things to be met on the road

than bogies. Run away now, and see that
the niggers are on hand when the stage
comes."

Two hours later the stage came with a
clatter of hoofs and a cloud of red dust,
which precipitated itself and a dozen thirsty
travelers upon the veranda before the hotel
bar-room; it brought also the usual " express " newspapers and much talk to Colonel
Swinger, who always received his guests in
a lofty personal fashion at the door, as he
might have done in his old Virginian home;
but it brought likewise — marvelous to re-
late — an *actual guest*, who had two trunks
and asked for a room! He was evidently a
stranger to the ways of Buena Vista, and
particularly to those of Colonel Swinger, and
at first seemed inclined to resent the social
attitude of his host, and his frank and free
curiosity. When he, however, found that
Colonel Swinger was even better satisfied to
give an account of *his own* affairs, his family, pedigree, and his present residence, he
began to betray some interest. The colonel
told him all the news, and would no doubt
have even expatiated on his ghostly visitant,
had he not prudently concluded that his

guest might decline to remain in a haunted inn. The stranger had spoken of staying a week ; he had some private mining speculations to watch at Wynyard's Gulch, — the next settlement, but he did not care to appear openly at the " Gulch Hotel." He was a man of thirty, with soft, pleasing features and a singular litheness of movement, which, combined with a nut-brown, gypsy complexion, at first suggested a foreigner. But his dialect, to the colonel's ears, was distinctly that of New England, and to this was added a puritanical and sanctimonious drawl. " He looked," said the colonel in after years, " like a blank light mulatter, but talked like a blank Yankee parson." For all that, he was acceptable to his host, who may have felt that his reminiscences of his plantation on the James River were palling on Buena Vista ears, and was glad of his new auditor. It was an advertisement, too, of the hotel, and a promise of its future fortunes. " Gentlemen having propahty interests at the Gulch, sah, prefer to stay at Buena Vista with another man of propahty, than to trust to those new-fangled papah-collared, gingerbread booths for traders that they call ' ho-

tels' there," he had remarked to some of
" the boys." In his preoccupation with the
new guest, he also became a little neglectful
of his old chum and dependent, Larry Hawkins. Nor was this the only circumstance
that filled the head of that shiftless loyal
retainer of the colonel with bitterness and
foreboding. Polly Swinger — the scornfully
indifferent, the contemptuously inaccessible,
the coldly capricious and petulant — was inclined to be polite to the stranger!

The fact was that Polly, after the fashion
of her sex, took it into her pretty head,
against all consistency and logic, suddenly
to make an exception to her general attitude
towards mankind in favor of one individual.
The reason-seeking masculine reader will
rashly conclude that this individual was the
cause as well as the object; but I am satisfied that every fair reader of these pages will
instinctively know better. Miss Polly had
simply selected the new guest, Mr. Starbuck,
to show *others*, particularly Larry Hawkins,
what she *could* do if she were inclined to be
civil. For two days she " fixed up " her distracting hair at him so that its silken floss
encircled her head like a nimbus ; she tucked

her oval chin into a white *fichu* instead of a
buttonless collar ; she appeared at dinner in
a newly starched yellow frock ! She talked
to him with " company manners ; " said she
would " admire to go to San Francisco," and
asked if he knew her old friends the Fauquier
girls from " Faginia." The colonel was somewhat disturbed ; he was glad that his daughter had become less negligent of her personal
appearance ; he could not but see, with the
others, how it enhanced her graces ; but he
was, with the others, not entirely satisfied
with her reasons. And he could not help
observing — what was more or less patent
to *all* — that Starbuck was far from being
equally responsive to her attentions, and at
times was indifferent and almost uncivil.
Nobody seemed to be satisfied with Polly's
transformation but herself.

But eventually she was obliged to assert
herself. The third evening after Starbuck's
arrival she was going over to the cabin of
Aunt Chloe, who not only did the washing
for Buena Vista, but assisted Polly in dress-
making. It was not far, and the night was
moonlit. As she crossed the garden she saw
Starbuck moving in the manzanita bushes

beyond; a mischievous light came into her eyes; she had not *expected* to meet him, but she had seen him go out, and there were always *possibilities*. To her surprise, however, he merely lifted his hat as she passed, and turned abruptly in another direction. This was more than the little heart-breaker of Buena Vista was accustomed to!

"Oh, Mr. Starbuck!" she called, in her laziest voice.

He turned almost impatiently.

"Since you're so civil and pressing, I thought I'd tell you I was just runnin' over to Aunt Chloe's," she said dryly.

"I should think it was hardly the proper thing for a young lady to do at this time of night," he said superciliously. "But you know best, — you know the people here."

Polly's cheeks and eyes flamed. "Yes, I reckon I do," she said crisply; "it's only a *stranger* here would think of being rude. Good-night, Mr. Starbuck!"

She tripped away after this Parthian shot, yet feeling, even in her triumph, that the conceited fool seemed actually relieved at her departure! And for the first time she now thought that she had seen something in his face that she did not like! But her lazy independence reasserted itself soon, and half an hour later, when she had left Aunt Chloe's cabin, she had regained her self-esteem. Yet, to avoid meeting him again, she took a longer route home, across the dried ditch and over the bluff, scarred by hydraulics, and so fell, presently, upon the old garden at the point where it adjoined the abandoned diggings. She was quite sure she had escaped a meeting with Starbuck, and was gliding along under the shadow of the pear-trees, when she suddenly stopped. An indescribable terror overcame her as she stared at a spot in the garden, perfectly illuminated by the moonlight not fifty yards from where she stood. For she saw on its surface a human head — a man's head! — seemingly on the level of the ground, staring in her direction. A hysterical laugh sprang from her lips, and she caught at the branches above her or she would have fallen! Yet in that moment the head had vanished! The moonlight revealed the empty garden, — the ground she had gazed at, — but nothing more!

She had never been superstitious. As a

child she had heard the negroes talk of " the hants," — that is, "the *haunts*" or spirits, — but had believed it a part of their ignorance, and unworthy a white child, — the daughter of their master ! She had laughed with Dick Ruggles over the illusions of Larry, and had shared her father's contemptuous disbelief of the wandering visitant being anything but a living man ; yet she would have screamed for assistance now, only for the greater fear of making her weakness known to Mr. Starbuck, and being dependent upon him for help.   And with it came the sudden conviction that *he* had seen this awful vision, too. This would account for his impatience of her presence and his rudeness.   She felt faint and giddy.   Yet after the first shock had passed, her old independence and pride came to her relief.   She would go to the spot and examine it.   If it were some trick or illusion, she would show her superiority and have the laugh on Starbuck.   She set her white teeth, clenched her little hands, and started out into the moonlight.   But alas ! for women's weakness.   The next moment she uttered a scream and almost fell into the arms of Mr. Starbuck, who had stepped out of the shadows beside her.

"So you see you *have* been frightened," he said, with a strange, forced laugh ; " but I warned you about going out alone ! "

Even in her fright she could not help seeing that he, too, seemed pale and agitated, at which she recovered her tongue and her self-possession.

" Anybody would be frightened by being dogged about under the trees," she said pertly.

" But you called out before you saw me," he said bluntly, " as if something had frightened you. That was *why* I came towards you."

She knew it was the truth ; but as she would not confess to her vision, she fibbed outrageously.

" Frightened," she said, with pale but lofty indignation. " What was there to frighten me ? I'm not a baby, to think I see a bogie in the dark! " This was said in the faint hope that *he* had seen something too. If it had been Larry or her father who had met her, she would have confessed everything.

" You had better go in," he said curtly. " I will see you safe inside the house."

She demurred at this, but as she could not persist in her first bold intention of examining the locality of the vision without admitting its existence, she permitted him to walk with her to the house, and then at once fled to her own room. Larry and her father noticed their entrance together and their agitated manner, and were uneasy. Yet the colonel's paternal pride and Larry's lover's respect kept the two men from communicating their thoughts to each other.

" The confounded pup has been tryin' to be familiar, and Polly's set him down," thought Larry, with glowing satisfaction.

" He's been trying some of his sanctimonious Yankee abolition talk on Polly, and she shocked him ! " thought the colonel exultingly.

But poor Polly had other things to think of in the silence of her room. Another woman would have unburdened herself to a confidante ; but Polly was too loyal to her father to shatter his beliefs, and too high-spirited to take another and a lesser person into her confidence. She was certain that Aunt Chloe would be full of sympathetic belief and speculations, but she would not trust a nigger with what she could n't tell her own father. For Polly really and truly believed that she had seen a ghost, no doubt the ghost of the murdered Sobriente, according to Larry's story. *Why* he should appear with only his head above ground puzzled her, although it suggested the Catholic idea of purgatory, and he was a Catholic! Perhaps he would have risen entirely but for that stupid Starbuck's presence; perhaps he had a message for *her* alone. The idea pleased Polly, albeit it was a " fearful joy " and attended with some cold shivering. Naturally, as a gentleman, he would appear to *her* — the daughter of a gentleman — the successor to his house — rather than to a Yankee stranger. What was she to do? For once her calm nerves were strangely thrilled; she could not think of undressing and going to bed, and two o'clock surprised her, still meditating, and occasionally peeping from her window upon the moonlit but vacant garden. If she saw him again, would she dare to go down alone? Suddenly she started to her feet with a beating heart! There was the unmistakable sound of a stealthy footstep in the passage, coming towards her room. Was it he ? In spite of her high resolves she felt that if the door opened she should scream ! She held her breath — the footsteps came nearer — were before her door — and *passed !*

Then it was that the blood rushed back to her cheek with a flush of indignation. Her room was at the end of the passage ; there was nothing beyond but a private staircase, long disused, except by herself, as a short cut through the old *patio* to the garden. No one else knew of it, and no one else had the right of access to it ! This insolent human intrusion — as she was satisfied it was now — overcame her fear, and she glided to the door. Opening it softly, she could hear the stealthy footsteps descending. She darted back, threw a shawl over her head and shoulders, and taking the small Derringer pistol which it had always been part of her ostentatious independence to place at her bed-head, she as stealthily followed the intruder. But the footsteps had died away before she reached the *patio*, and she saw only the small deserted, grass-grown courtyard, half hidden in shadows, in whose centre stood the fateful and long sealed-up well! A shudder came over her at again being brought into contact with the cause of her frightful vision, but as her eyes became accustomed to the darkness, she saw something more real and appalling! The well was no longer sealed! Fragments of bricks and boards lay around it! One end of a rope, coiled around it like a huge snake, descended its foul depths; and as she gazed with staring eyes, the head and shoulders of a man emerged slowly from it! But it was *not* the ghostly apparition of last evening, and her terror changed to scorn and indignation as she recognized the face of Starbuck!

Their eyes met; an oath broke from his lips. He made a movement to spring from the well, but as the girl started back, the pistol held in her hand was discharged aimlessly in the air, and the report echoed throughout the courtyard. With a curse Starbuck drew back, instantly disappeared in the well, and Polly fell fainting on the steps. When she came to, her father and Larry were at her side. They had been alarmed at the report, and had rushed quickly to the *patio*, but not in time to prevent the

escape of Starbuck and his accomplice. By
the time she had recovered her consciousness,
they had learned the full extent of that extraordinary revelation which she had so in-
nocently precipitated. Sobriente's well had
really concealed a rich gold ledge, — actually
tunneled and galleried by him secretly in
the past, — and its only other outlet was an
opening in the garden hidden by a stone
which turned on a swivel. Its existence had
been unknown to Sobriente's successor, but
was known to the Kanaka who had worked
with Sobriente, who fled with his daughter
after the murder, but who no doubt was
afraid to return and work the mine. He
had imparted the secret to Starbuck, another
half-breed, son of a Yankee missionary and
Hawaiian wife, who had evidently conceived
this plan of seeking Buena Vista with an
accomplice, and secretly removing such gold
as was still accessible. The accomplice,
afterwards identified by Larry as the wandering tramp, failed to discover the secret
entrance *from* the garden, and Starbuck was
consequently obliged to attempt it from the
hotel — for which purpose he had introduced himself as a boarder — by opening

the disused well secretly at night. These facts were obtained from papers found in the otherwise valueless trunks, weighted with stones for ballast, which Starbuck had brought to the hotel to take away his stolen treasure in, but which he was obliged to leave in his hurried flight. The attempt would have doubtless succeeded but for Polly's courageous and timely interference !

And now that they had told her *all*, they only wanted to know what had first excited *her* suspicions, and driven her to seek the well as the object of Starbuck's machinations? *They* had noticed her manner when she entered the house that night, and Starbuck's evident annoyance. Had she taxed him with her suspicions, and so discovered a clue ?

It was a terrible temptation to Polly to pose as a more perfect heroine, and one may not blame her if she did not rise entirely superior to it. Her previous belief, that the head of the accomplice at the opening of the garden was that of a *ghost*, she now felt was certainly in the way, as was also her conduct to Starbuck, whom she believed to be equally frightened, and whom she never once suspected ! So she said, with a certain lofty simplicity, that there were *some things* which she really did not care to talk about, and Larry and her father left her that night with the firm conviction that the rascal Starbuck had tried to tempt her to fly with him and his riches, and had been crushingly foiled. Polly never denied this, and once, in later days, when admiringly taxed with it by Larry, she admitted with dove-like simplicity that she *may* have been too foolishly polite to her father's guest for the sake of her father's hotel.

However, all this was of small account to the thrilling news of a new discovery and working of the " old gold ledge " at Buena Vista ! As the three kept their secret from the world, the discovery was accepted in the neighborhood as the result of careful examination and prospecting on the part of Colonel Swinger and his partner Larry Hawkins. And when the latter gentleman afterwards boldly proposed to Polly Swinger, she mischievously declared that she accepted him only that the secret might not go " out of the family."

LIBERTY JONES'S DISCOVERY

I⊤ was at best merely a rocky trail wind-
ing along a shelf of the eastern slope of
the Santa Cruz range, yet the only road between the sea and the inland valley. The
hoof-prints of a whole century of zigzagging
mules were impressed on the soil, regularly
soaked by winter rains and dried by summer
suns during that period; the occasional ruts
of heavy, rude, wooden wheels — long ob-
solete — were still preserved and visible.
Weather-worn boulders and ledges, lying in
the unclouded glare of an August sky, radi-
ated a quivering heat that was intolerable,
even while above them the masts of gigantic
pines rocked their tops in the cold southwestern trades from the unseen ocean beyond. A red, burning dust lay everywhere,
as if the heat were slowly and visibly pre-
cipitating itself.

The creaking of wheels and axles, the
muffled plunge of hoofs, and the cough of
a horse in the dust thus stirred presently

broke the profound woodland silence. Then
a dirty white canvas-covered emigrant wagon
slowly arose with the dust along the ascent.
It was travel-stained and worn, and with its
rawboned horses seemed to have reached the
last stage of its journey and fitness. The
only occupants, a man and a girl, appeared
to be equally jaded and exhausted, with the
added querulousness of discontent in their
sallow and badly nourished faces. Their
voices, too, were not unlike the creaking
they had been pitched to overcome, and
there was an absence of reserve and consciousness in their speech, which told pathetically of an equal absence of society.

"It's no user talkin'! I tell ye, ye hain't
got no more sense than a coyote! I'm sick
and tired of it, doggoned if I ain't! Ye
ain't no more use nor a hossfly, — and jest
ez hinderin'! It was along o' you that we
lost the stock at Laramie, and ef ye'd bin
at all decent and takin', we'd hev had kempany that helped, instead of laggin' on yere
alone!"

"What did ye bring me for?" retorted
the girl shrilly. "I might hev stayed with
Aunt Marty. I wasn't hankerin' to come."

"Bring ye for?" repeated her father contemptuously; "I reckoned ye might be o' some account here, whar wimmin folks is skeerce, in the way o' helpin', — and mebbe gettin' yer married to some likely feller. Mighty much chance o' that, with yer yaller face and skin and bones."

"Ye can't blame me for takin' arter you, dad," she said, with a shrill laugh, but no other resentment of his brutality.

"Ye want somebody to take arter you — with a club," he retorted angrily. "Ye hear! Wot's that ye're doin' now?"

She had risen and walked to the tail of the wagon. "Goin' to get out and walk. I'm tired o' bein' jawed at."

She jumped into the road. The act was neither indignant nor vengeful; the frequency of such scenes had blunted their sting. She was probably "tired" of the quarrel, and ended it rudely. Her father, however, let fly a Parthian arrow.

"Ye need n't think I 'm goin' to wait for ye, ez I hev! Ye 've got to keep tetch with the team, or get left. And a good riddance of bad rubbidge."

In reply the girl dived into the underwood

beside the trail, picked a wild berry or two,
stripped a wand of young hazel she had
broken off, and switching it at her side,
skipped along on the outskirts of the wood
and ambled after the wagon. Seen in the
full, merciless glare of a Californian sky,
she justified her father's description; thin
and bony, her lank frame outstripped the
body of her ragged calico dress, which was
only kept on her shoulders by straps, — possibly her father's cast-off braces. A boy's
soft felt hat covered her head, and shadowed
her only notable feature, a pair of large
dark eyes, looking larger for the hollow
temples which narrowed the frame in which
they were set.

So long as the wagon crawled up the ascent the girl knew she could easily keep up
with it, or even distance the tired horses.
She made one or two incursions into the
wood, returning like an animal from quest
of food, with something in her mouth, which
she was tentatively chewing, and once only
with some inedible *mandrono* berries, plucked
solely for their brilliant coloring. It was
very hot and singularly close; the higher
current of air had subsided, and, looking

up, a singular haze seemed to have taken its
place between the treetops. Suddenly she
heard a strange, rumbling sound; an odd
giddiness overtook her, and she was obliged
to clutch at a sapling to support herself;
she laughed vacantly, though a little frightened, and looked vaguely towards the summit of the road; but the wagon had already disappeared. A strange feeling of
nausea then overcame her; she spat out the
leaves she had been chewing, disgustedly.
But the sensation as quickly passed, and
she once more sought the trail and began
slowly to follow the tracks of the wagon.
The air blew freshly, the treetops began
again to rock over her head, and the incident was forgotten.

Presently she paused; she must have
missed the trail, for the wagon tracks had
ended abruptly before a large boulder that
lay across the mountain trail. She dipped
into the woods again; here there were other
wagon tracks that confused her. It was
like her dogged, stupid father to miss the
trail; she felt a gleam of malicious satisfaction at his discomfiture. Sooner or later, he
would have to retrace his steps and virtually

come back for her! She took up a position where two rough wheel ruts and tracks intersected each other, one of which must be the missing trail. She noticed, too, the broader hoof-prints of cattle without the following wheel ruts, and instead of traces, the long smooth trails made by the dragging of logs, and knew by these tokens that she must be near the highway or some woodman's hut or ranch. She began to be thirsty, and was glad, presently, when her quick, rustic ear caught the tinkling of water. Yet it was not so easy to discover, and she was getting footsore and tired again before she found it, some distance away, in a gully coming from a fissure in a dislocated piece of outcrop. It was beautifully clear, cold, and sparkling, with a slightly sweetish taste, yet unlike the brackish " alkali " of the plains. It refreshed and soothed her greatly, so much that, reclining against a tree, but where she would be quite visible from the trail, her eyes closed dreamily, and presently she slept.

When she awoke, the shafts of sunlight were striking almost level into her eyes. She must have slept two hours. Her father had not returned; she knew the passage of the wagon would have awakened her. She began to feel strange, but not yet alarmed; it was only the uncertainty that made her uneasy. Had her father really gone on by some other trail? Or had he really hurried on and left her, as he said he would? The thought brought an odd excitement to her rather than any fear. A sudden sense of freedom, as if some galling chain had dropped from her, sent a singular thrill through her frame. Yet she felt confused with her independence, not knowing what to do with it, and momentarily dazzled with the possible gift.

At this moment she heard voices, and the figures of two men appeared on the trail.

They were talking earnestly, and walking as if familiar with the spot, yet gazing around them as if at some novelty of the aspect.

" And look there," said one; " there has been some serious disturbance of that outcrop," pointing in the direction of the spring; " the lower part has distinctly subsided." He spoke with a certain authority, and dominance of position, and was evidently the superior, as he was the elder of the two, although both were roughly dressed.

"Yes, it does kinder look as if it had lost its holt, like the ledge yonder."

"And you see I am right; the movement was from east to west," continued the elder man.

The girl could not comprehend what they said, and even thought them a little silly. But she advanced towards them; at which they stopped short, staring at her. With feminine instinct she addressed the more important one : —

"Ye ain't passed no wagon nor team goin' on, hev ye?"

"What sort of wagon?" said the man.

"Em'grant wagon, two yaller hosses. Old man — my dad — drivin'." She added the latter kinship as a protecting influence against strangers, in spite of her previous independence.

The men glanced at each other.

"How long ago?"

The girl suddenly remembered that she had slept two hours.

"Sens noon," she said hesitatingly.

" Since the earthquake ? "

" Wot 's that ? "

The man came impatiently towards her.
" How did you come here? "

" Got outer the wagon to walk. I
reckon dad missed the trail, and hez got
off somewhere where I can't find him."

" What trail was he on, — where was he
going? "

" Sank Hozay,[1] I reckon. He was goin'
up the grade — side o' the hill; he must
hev turned off where there 's a big rock
hangin' over."

" Did you *see* him turn off? "

" No."

The second man, who was in hearing distance, had turned away, and was ostentatiously examining the sky and the treetops;
the man who had spoken to her joined him,
and they said something in a low voice.
They turned again and came slowly towards
her. She, from some obscure sense of imitation, stared at the treetops and the sky
as the second man had done. But the first
man now laid his hand kindly on her shoulder and said, " Sit down."

[1] San José.

Then they told her there had been an earthquake so strong that it had thrown down a part of the hillside, including the wagon trail. That a wagon team and driver, such as she had described, had been carried down with it, crushed to fragments, and buried under a hundred feet of rock in the gulch below. A party had gone down to examine, but it would be weeks perhaps before they found it, and she must be prepared for the worst. She looked at them vaguely and with tearless eyes.

"Then ye reckon dad's dead?"

"We fear it."

"Then wot's a-goin' to become o' me?" she said simply.

They glanced again at each other. "Have you no friends in California?" said the elder man.

"Nary one."

"What was your father going to do?"

"Dunno. I reckon *he* did n't either."

"You may stay here for the present," said the elder man meditatively. "Can you milk?"

The girl nodded. "And I suppose you know something about looking after stock?" he continued.

The girl remembered that her father thought she did n't, but this was no time for criticism, and she again nodded.

" Come with me," said the older man, rising. " I suppose," he added, glancing at her ragged frock, " everything you have is in the wagon."

She nodded, adding with the same cold *naïveté*, " It ain't much ! "

They walked on, the girl following ; at times straying furtively on either side, as if meditating an escape in the woods, — which indeed had once or twice been vaguely in her thoughts, — but chiefly to avoid further questioning and not to hear what the men said to each other. For they were evidently speaking of her, and she could not help hearing the younger repeat her words, " Wot 's a-goin' to become o' me ? " with considerable amusement, and the addition : " She 'll take care of herself, you bet ! I call that remark o' hers the richest thing out."

" And *I* call the state of things that provoked it — monstrous ! " said the elder man grimly. " You don't know the lives of these people."

Presently they came to an open clearing

in the forest, yet so incomplete that many of the felled trees, partly lopped of their boughs, still lay where they had fallen. There was a cabin or dwelling of unplaned, unpainted boards; very simple in structure, yet made in a workmanlike fashion, quite unlike the usual log cabin she had seen. This made her think that the elder man was a " towny," and not a frontiersman like the other.

As they approached the cabin the elder man stopped, and turning to her, said : —

" Do you know Indians ? "

The girl started, and then recovering herself with a quick laugh: " G'lang ! — there ain't any Injins here ! "

" Not the kind *you* mean ; these are very peaceful. There's a squaw here whom you will " — he stopped, hesitated as he looked critically at the girl, and then corrected himself — " who will help you."

He pushed open the cabin door and showed an interior, equally simple but well joined and fitted, — a marvel of neatness and finish to the frontier girl's eye. There were shelves and cupboards and other conveniences, yet with no ostentation of refinement to frighten her rustic sensibilities.

Then he pushed open another door leading into a shed and called "Waya." A stout, undersized Indian woman, fitted with a coarse cotton gown, but cleaner and more presentable than the girl's one frock, appeared in the doorway. "This is Waya, who attends to the cooking and cleaning," he said; "and by the way, what is your name?"

"Libby Jones."

He took a small memorandum book and a "stub" of pencil from his pocket. "Elizabeth Jones," he said, writing it down. The girl interposed a long red hand.

"No," she interrupted sharply, "not Elizabeth, but Libby, — short for Lib'rty."

"Liberty?"

"Yes."

"Liberty Jones, then. Well, Waya, this is Miss Jones, who will look after the cows and calves — and the dairy." Then glancing at her torn dress, he added: "You'll find some clean things in there, until I can send up something from San José. Waya will show you."

Without further speech he turned away with the other man. When they were some distance from the cabin, the younger remarked : —

"More like a boy than a girl, ain't she?"

"So much the better for her work," returned the elder grimly.

"I reckon! I was only thinkin' she did n't han'some much either as a boy or girl, eh, doctor?" he pursued.

"Well! as *that* won't make much difference to the cows, calves, or the dairy, it need n't trouble *us*," returned the doctor dryly. But here a sudden outburst of laughter from the cabin made them both turn in that direction. They were in time to see Liberty Jones dancing out of the cabin door in a large cotton pinafore, evidently belonging to the squaw, who was following her with half - laughing, half-frightened expostulations. The two men stopped and gazed at the spectacle.

" Do n't seem to be takin' the old man's death very pow'fully," said the younger, with a laugh.

" Quite as much as he deserved, I daresay," said the doctor curtly. "If the accident had happened to *her*, he would have whined and whimpered to us for the sake of getting something, but have been as much relieved, you may be certain. *She's* too young and too natural to be a hypocrite yet."

Suddenly the laughter ceased and Liberty Jones's voice arose, shrill but masterful: "Thar, that'll do! Quit now! You jest get back to your scrubbin' — d' ye hear? I'm boss o' this shanty, you bet!"

The doctor turned with a grim smile to his companion. "That's the only thing that bothered me, and I've been waiting for. She's settled it. She'll do. Come."

They turned away briskly through the wood. At the end of half an hour's walk they found the team that had brought them there in waiting, and drove towards San José. It was nearly ten miles before they passed another habitation or trace of clearing. And by this time night had fallen upon the cabin they had left, and upon the newly made orphan and her Indian companion, alone and contented in that trackess solitude.

.   .   .   .

Liberty Jones had been a year at the cabin. In that time she had learned that her employer's name was Doctor Ruysdael, that he had a lucrative practice in San José, but had also " taken up " a league or two of wild forest land in the Santa Cruz range, which he preserved and held after a fashion of his own, which gave him the reputation of being a " crank " among the very few neighbors his vast possessions permitted, and the equally few friends his singular tastes allowed him. It was believed that a man owning such an enormous quantity of timber land, who should refuse to set up a sawmill and absolutely forbid the felling of trees ; who should decline to connect it with the highway to Santa Cruz, and close it against improvement and speculation, had given sufficient evidence of his insanity ; but when to this was added the rumor that he himself was not only devoid of the human instinct of hunting the wild animals with which his domain abounded, but that he held it so sacred to their use as to forbid the firing of a gun within his limits, and that these restrictions were further preserved and " policed " by the scattered remnants of a band of aborigines, — known as "digger Injins," — it was seriously hinted that his eccentricity had acquired a political and moral significance, and demanded legislative interference. But the doctor was a rich man, a necessity to his patients, a good marksman, and, it was rumored, did not include his fellow men among the animals he had a distaste for killing.

Of all this, however, Liberty knew little and cared less. The solitude appealed to her sense of freedom ; she did not " hanker " after a society she had never known. At the end of the first week, when the doctor communicated to her briefly, by letter, the convincing proofs of the death of her father and his entombment beneath the sunken cliff, she accepted the fact without comment or apparent emotion. Two months later, when her only surviving relative, " Aunt Marty," of Missouri, acknowledged the news — communicated by Doctor Ruysdael — with Scriptural quotations and the cheerful hope that it " would be a lesson to her " and she would " profit in her new place," she left her aunt's letter unanswered.

She looked after the cows and calves with an interest that was almost possessory, patronized and played with the squaw, — yet made her feel her inferiority, — and moved among the peaceful aborigines with the domination of a white woman and a superior. She tolerated the half-monthly visits of "Jim Hoskins," the young companion of the doctor, who she learned was the doctor's factor and overseer of the property, who lived seven miles away on an agricultural clearing, and whose control of her actions was evidently limited by the doctor, — for the doctor's sake alone. Nor was Mr. Hoskins inclined to exceed those limits. He looked upon her as something abnormal, — a "crank" as remarkable in her way as her patron was in his, neuter of sex and vague of race, and he simply restricted his supervision to the bringing and taking of messages. She remained sole queen of the domain. A rare straggler from the main road, penetrating this seclusion, might have scarcely distinguished her from Waya, in her coarse cotton gown and slouched hat, except for the free stride which contrasted with her companion's waddle. Once, in following an estrayed calf, she had crossed the highway and been saluted by a passing teamster in the digger dialect; yet the mistake left no sting in her memory. And, like the digger, she shrank from that civilization which had only proved a hard taskmaster.

The sole touch of human interest she had in her surroundings was in the rare visits of the doctor and his brief but sincere commendation of her rude and rustic work. It is possible that the strange, middle-aged, gray-haired, intellectual man, whose very language was at times mysterious and unintelligible to her, and whose suggestion of power awed her, might have touched some untried filial chord in her being. Although she felt that, save for absolute freedom, she was little more to him than she had been to her father, yet he had never told her she had " no sense," that she was " a hindrance," and he had even praised her performance of her duties. Eagerly as she looked for his coming, in his actual presence she felt a singular uneasiness of which she was not entirely ashamed, and if she was relieved at his departure, it none the less left her to a delightful memory of him, a warm sense of

his approval, and a fierce ambition to be
worthy of it, for which she would have sac-
rificed herself or the other miserable retain-
ers about her, as a matter of course. She
had driven Waya and the other squaws far
along the sparse tableland pasture in search
of missing stock; she herself had lain out
all night on the rocks beside an ailing
heifer. Yet, while satisfied to earn his
praise for the performance of her duty, for
some feminine reason she thought more fre-
quently of a casual remark he had made
on his last visit: "You are stronger and
more healthy in this air," he had said, looking critically into her face. "We have got
that abominable alkali out of your system,
and wholesome food will do the rest." She
was not sure she had quite understood him,
but she remembered that she had felt her
face grow hot when he spoke, — perhaps because she had not understood him.

His next visit was a day or two delayed,
and in her anxiety she had ventured as far
as the highway to earnestly watch for his
coming. From her hiding-place in the underwood she could see the team and Jim
Hoskins already waiting for him. Presently

she saw him drive up to the trail in a carry-
all with a party of ladies and gentlemen.
He alighted, bade " Good-by " to the party,
and the team turned to retrace its course.
But in that single moment she had been
struck and bewildered by what seemed to
her the dazzlingly beautiful apparel of the
women, and their prettiness. She felt a sudden consciousness of her own coarse, shapeless calico gown, her straggling hair, and her
felt hat, and a revulsion of feeling seized her.
She crept like a wounded animal out of the
underwood, and then ran swiftly and almost
fiercely back towards the cabin. She ran
so fast that for a time she almost kept pace
with the doctor and Hoskins in the wagon
on the distant trail. Then she dived into
the underwood again, and making a short
cut through the forest, came at the end of
two hours within hailing distance of the
cabin, — footsore and exhausted, in spite of
the strange excitement that had driven her
back. Here she thought she heard voices —
his voice among the rest — calling her, but
the same singular revulsion of feeling hurried her vaguely on again, even while she
experienced a foolish savage delight in not

answering the summons. In this erratic wandering she came upon the spring she had found on her first entrance in the forest a year ago, and drank feverishly a second time at its trickling source. She could see that since her first visit it had worn a great hollow below the tree roots and now formed a shining, placid pool. As she stooped to look at it, she suddenly observed that it reflected her whole figure as in a cruel mirror, — her slouched hat and loosened hair, her coarse and shapeless gown, her hollow cheeks and dry yellow skin, — in all their hopeless, uncompromising details. She uttered a quick, angry, half-reproachful cry, and turned again to fly. But she had not gone far before she came upon the hurrying figures and anxious faces of the doctor and Hoskins. She stopped, trembling and irresolute.

"Ah," said the doctor, in a tone of frank relief. "Here you are! I was getting worried about you. Waya said you had been gone since morning!" He stopped and looked at her attentively. "Is anything the matter?"

His evident concern sent a warm glow over her chilly frame, and yet the strange sensation remained. " No — no! " she stammered.

Doctor Ruysdael turned to Hoskins. " Go back and tell Waya I 've found her."

Libby felt that the doctor only wanted to get rid of his companion, and became awed again.

" Has anybody been bothering you ? "

" No."

" Have the diggers frightened you ? "

" No " — with a gesture of contempt.

" Have you and Waya quarreled ? "

" Nary " — with a faint, tremulous smile.

He still stared at her, and then dropped his blue eyes musingly. " Are you lonely here ? Would you rather go to San José ? "

Like a flash the figures of the two smartly dressed women started up before her again, with every detail of their fresh and wholesome finery as cruelly distinct as had been her own shapeless ugliness in the mirror of the spring. " No! *No!* " she broke out vehemently and passionately. " Never! "

He smiled gently. " Look here! I 'll send you up some books. You read — don't you ? " She nodded quickly. " Some magazines and papers. Odd I never thought of it before," he added half musingly. "Come along to the cabin. And," he stopped again and said decisively, "the next time you want anything, don't wait for me to come, but write."

A few days after he left she received a package of books, — an odd collection of novels, magazines, and illustrated journals of the period. She received them eagerly as an evidence of his concern for her, but it is to be feared that her youthful nature found little satisfaction in the gratification of fancy. Many of the people she read of were strange to her; many of the incidents related seemed to her mere lies; some tales which treated of people in her own sphere she found profoundly uninteresting. In one of the cheaper magazines she chanced upon a fashion plate; she glanced eagerly through all the others for a like revelation until she got a dozen together, when she promptly relegated the remaining literature to a corner and oblivion. The text accompanying the plates was in a jargon not always clear, but her instinct supplied the rest. She dispatched by Hoskins a note to Doctor Ruysdael: "Please send me some brite kalikers

and things for sewing. You told me to
ask." A few days later brought the re-
sponse in a good-sized parcel.

Yet this did not keep her from her care
of the stock nor her rambles in the forest;
she was quick to utilize her rediscovery of
the spring for watering the cattle; it was
not so far afield as the half-dried creek in
the cañon, and was a quiet sylvan spot.
She ate her frugal midday meal there and
drank of its waters, and, secure in her seclusion, bathed there and made her rude
toilet when the cows were driven home.
But she did not again look into its mirrored
surface when it was tranquil!

And so a month passed. But when Doctor Ruysdael was again due at the cabin, a
letter was brought by Hoskins, with the
news that he was called away on professional
business down the coast, and could not come
until two weeks later. In the disappoint-
ment that overcame her, she did not at first
notice that Hoskins was gazing at her with
a singular expression, which was really one
of undisguised admiration. Never having
seen this before in the eyes of any man who
looked at her, she referred it to some vague

"larking" or jocularity, for which she was in no mood.

"Say, Libby! you 're gettin' to be a right smart-lookin' gal. Seems to agree with ye up here," said Hoskins with an awkward laugh. "Darned ef ye ain't lookin' awful purty!"

"G'long!" said Liberty Jones, more than ever convinced of his badinage.

"Fact," said Hoskins energetically. "Why, Doc would tell ye so, too. See ef he don't!"

At this Liberty Jones felt her face grow hot. "You jess get!" she said, turning away in as much embarrassment as anger. Yet he hovered near her with awkward attentions that pleased while it still angered her. He offered to go with her to look up the cows; she flatly declined, yet with a strange satisfaction in his evident embarrassment. This may have lent some animation to her face, for he drew a long breath and said : —

"Don't go pertendin' ye don't know yer purty. Say, let me and you walk a bit and have a talk together." But Libby had another idea in her mind and curtly dismissed him. Then she ran swiftly to the spring,

for the words " The Doc will tell ye so, too"
were ringing in her ears. The doctor who
came with the two beautifully dressed women! *he* — would tell her she was pretty!
She had not dared to look at herself in that
crystal mirror since that dreadful day two
months ago. She would now.

It was a pretty place in the cool· shade of
the giant trees, and the hoof-marks of cattle
drinking from the run beneath the pool had
not disturbed the margin of that tranquil
sylvan basin. For a moment she stood
tremulous and uncertain, and then going up
to the shining mirror, dropped on her knees
before it with her thin red hands clasped
on her lap. Unconsciously she had taken
the attitude of prayer; perhaps there was
something like it in her mind.

And then the light glanced full on the
figure that she saw there !

It fell on a full oval face and throat guile-
less of fleck or stain, smooth as a' child's and
glowing with health; on large dark eyes, no
longer sunk in their orbits, but filled with
an eager, happy light; on bared arms now
shapely in contour and cushioned with firm
flesh; on a dazzling smile, the like of which

had never been on the face of Liberty Jones
before !

She rose to her feet, and yet lingered as
if loath to part from this delightful vision.
Then a fear overcame her that it was some
trick of the water, and she sped swiftly back
to the house to consult the little mirror
which hung in her sleeping-room, but which
she had never glanced at since the momen-
tous day of the spring. She took it shyly
into the sunshine, and found that it corroborated the reflection of the spring. That
night she worked until late at the calico Doctor Ruysdael had sent her, and went to bed
happy. The next day brought her Hoskins
again with a feeble excuse of inquiring if
she had a letter for the doctor, and she was
surprised to find that he was reinforced by
a stranger from Hoskins's farm, who was
equally awkward and vaguely admiring.
But the appearance of the *two* men produced
a singular phase in her impressions and experience. She was no longer indignant at
Hoskins, but she found relief in accepting
the compliments of the stranger in prefer-
ence, and felt a delight in Hoskins's discomfiture. Waya, promoted to the burlesque

of a chaperone, grinned with infinite delight and understanding.

When at last the day came for the doctor's arrival, he was duly met by Hoskins, and as duly informed by that impressible subordinate of the great change in Liberty's appearance. But the doctor was far from being equally impressed with his factor's story, and indeed showed much more interest in the appearance of the stock which they met along the road. Once the doctor got out of the wagon to inspect a cow, and particularly the coat of a rough draught horse that had been turned out and put under Liberty's care. " His skin is like velvet," said the doctor. " The girl evidently understands stock, and knows how to keep them in condition."

" I reckon she 's beginning to understand herself, too," said Hoskins. " Golly ! wait till ye see *her*."

The doctor *did* see her, but with what feelings he did not as frankly express. She was not at the cabin when they arrived, but presently appeared from the direction of the spring where, for reasons of her own, she had evidently made her toilet. Doctor Ruys-

dael was astounded; Hoskins's praise was
not exaggerated; and there was an added
charm that Hoskins was not prepared for.
She had put on a gown of her own making,
— the secret toil of many a long night, —
amateurishly fashioned from some cheap
yellow calico the doctor had sent her, yet fitting her wonderfully, and showing every
curve of her graceful figure. Unaccented
by a corset, — an article she had never
known, — even the lines of the stiff, unyield-
ing calico had a fashion that was nymph-
like and suited her unfettered limbs. Doctor
Ruysdael was profoundly moved. Though
a philosopher, he was practical. He found
himself suddenly confronted not only by a
beautiful girl, but a problem! It was impossible to keep the existence of this woodland nymph from the knowledge of his distant neighbors; it was equally impossible
for him to assume the responsibility of keeping a goddess like this in her present position. He had noticed her previous improvement, but had never dreamed that pure and
wholesome living could in two months work
such a miracle. And he was to a certain
degree responsible; *he* had created her, — a

beautiful Frankenstein, whose lustrous, appealing eyes were even now menacing his security and position.

Perhaps she saw trouble and perplexity in the face where she had expected admiration and pleasure, for a slight chill went over her as he quickly praised the appearance of the stock and spoke of her own improvement. But when they were alone, he turned to her abruptly.

" You said you had no wish to go to San José? "

" No." Yet she was conscious that her greatest objection had been removed, and she colored faintly.

" Listen to me," he said dryly. " You deserve a better position than this, — a better home and surroundings than you have here. You are older, too, — a woman almost, — and you must look ahead."

A look of mingled fright, reproach, and appeal came into her eloquent face. " Yer wantin' to send me away? " she stammered.

" No," he said frankly. " It is you who are *growing* away. This is no longer the place for you."

" But I want to stay. I don't wanter go. I am — I *was* happy here,"

" But I 'm thinking of giving up this place. It takes up too much of my time. You must be provided " —

" *You* are going away? " she said passionately.

" Yes."

" Take me with you. I 'll go anywhere! — to San José — wherever you go. Don't turn me off as dad did, for I 'll foller you as I never followed dad. I 'll go with you — or I 'll die! "

There was neither fear nor shame in her words; it was the outspoken instinct of the animal he had been rearing; he was convinced and appalled by it.

" I am returning to San José at once," he said gravely. " You shall go with me — *for the present!* Get yourself ready! "

He took her to San José, and temporarily to the house of a patient, — a widow lady, — while he tried, alone, to grapple with the problem that now confronted him. But that problem became more complicated at the end of the third day, by Liberty Jones falling suddenly and alarmingly ill. The symptoms were so grave that the doctor, in his anxiety, called in a brother physician in consultation. When the examination was over, the two men withdrew and stared at each other.

" Of course there is no doubt that the symptoms all point to slow arsenical poisoning," said the consulting doctor.

" Yes," said Ruysdael quickly, " yet it is utterly inexplicable, both as to motive and opportunity."

" Humph ! " said the other grimly, "young ladies take arsenic in minute doses to improve the complexion and promote tissue, forgetting that the effects are cumulative when they stop suddenly. Your young friend has ' sworn off ' too quickly."

" But it is impossible," said Doctor Ruysdael impatiently. " She is a mere child — a country girl — ignorant of such habits."

" Humph ! the peasants in the Tyrol try it on themselves after noticing the effect on the coats of cattle."

Doctor Ruysdael started. A recollection of the sleek draught horse flashed upon him. He rose and hastily reëntered the patient's room. In a few moments he returned. " Do you think I could remove her at once to the mountains ? " he said gravely.

"Yes, with care and a return to graduated doses of the same poison ; you know it's the only remedy just now," answered the other.

By noon the next day the doctor and his patient had returned to the cabin, but Ruysdael himself carried the helpless Liberty Jones to the spring and deposited her gently beside it. "You may drink now," he said gravely.

The girl did so eagerly, apparently imbibing new strength from the sparkling water. The doctor meanwhile coolly filled a phial from the same source, and made a hasty test of the contents by the aid of some other phials from his case. The result seemed to satisfy him. Then he said gravely :

"And *this* is the spring you had discovered?"

The girl nodded.

"And you and the cattle have daily used it?"

She nodded again wonderingly. Then she caught his hand appealingly.

"You won't send me away?"

He smiled oddly as he glanced from the waters of the hill to the brimming eyes. "No."

" No-r," tremulously, " go away — your-self ? "

The doctor looked this time only into her eyes. There was a tremendous idea in his own, which seemed in some way to have solved that dreadful problem.

" No! We will stay here *together.*"

.   .   .   .

Six months later there was a paragraph in the San Francisco press: " The wonderful Arsenical Spring in the Santa Cruz Mountain, known as 'Liberty Spring,' discovered by Doctor Ruysdael, has proved such a remarkable success that we understand the temporary huts for patients are to be shortly replaced by a magnificent Spa Hotel worthy of the spot, and the eligible villa sites it has brought into the market. It will be a source of pleasure to all to know that the beautiful nymph — a worthy successor to the far-famed 'Elise' of the German 'Brunnen' — who has administered the waters to so many grateful patients will still be in attendance, although it is rumored that she is shortly to become the wife of the distinguished discoverer."

ELECTROTYPED AND PRINTED
BY H. O. HOUGHTON AND CO.

The Riverside Press

CAMBRIDGE, MASS., U. S. A.